# Technology vs The Witches

## and other strange tales

Edwin Hird

Copyright © 2024 Edwin Hird

All rights reserved

TECHNOLOGY VS THE WITCHES AND OTHER STRANGE TALES

First edition January 2024

This is a work of fiction. Names, characters, places, events and dialogue are either drawn from the author's imagination or are used in a fictitious manner. Any similarity to actual events or persons, living or dead, is entirely coincidental.

No part of this book may be reproduced in any form or by any electronic or mechanical means without written permission from the author, except for the use of brief quotations in a book review.

This book is suitable for general reading but contains events some readers might find unsettling. Contains mild profanities.

Thanks to Alex for technical advice, and to Joyce for putting up with me while I wrote this book.

# Technology vs The Witches

## and other strange tales

### Contents

| | |
|---|---|
| Technology vs The Witches | Page 3 |
| The Monastery | Page 55 |
| Best Served Cold | Page 100 |
| The Hospitals | Page 137 |
| The Winter Wedding | Page 166 |
| The Dark Side | Page 225 |

# Technology vs The Witches

## Chapter 1

Doris was looking through drawers and cupboards, getting increasingly exasperated. Eventually she threw herself onto a chair and wiped the sweat from her brow.

"Agnes!" she called to her sister. "Have you been using my eye of toad?"

"Certainly not!" Agnes answered indignantly as she entered the room. "I never touch the stuff. I always leave that sort of thing to you."

"Well, I can't find it anywhere and I know for a fact last time I used it there were at least three left in the jar. Do you think eye of frog will do instead?"

"Not my area of expertise, dear," Agnes replied shaking her head. "Definitely your department."

"Bother! I'll give it a go and see what happens. And next time you're out foraging keep your eyes open. Here's a jar in case you see any." She passed her sister a small glass jar, which Agnes put into the front pocket of her apron.

"Will do. What are you making?"

"Fertiliser. One of the young women in the village isn't managing to conceive."

"Well, you've never failed before."

"No, but I've never had to use eye of frog instead of eye of toad before either. It might work, with a bit of luck."

"I have faith in you and your potions, dear. Oh! What's that noise?"

There was a tapping sound, which came from the window. Doris looked out but couldn't see anyone. She opened the door and there on the step were two crows. One was carrying a small green package, about the size of an adult rat, and looked tired from the weight. It dropped the package and looked up at Doris.

"Oh, come on in! Come on in! Quick, Agnes, get them some water and a biscuit or something. The poor things are worn out!"

Agnes brought a little dish of water, a biscuit and a piece of bread, which were quickly devoured. Doris picked up the package while Agnes fussed over the birds. She carefully unfolded it; it was a rubbery leaf, about the size of a dinner plate, with words etched into the surface on one side. As she read it her expression changed.

"Oh, dear," she said slowly. "We've been summoned. The Fern wants to see us immediately."

Agnes too looked solemn. "Why? What have we done? Surely she can't have a job for us, not at our age. I thought she was giving all the important jobs to the youngsters."

"It doesn't say. Just says she needs to see us as soon as we can get there."

"Well, at least it's a warm day. All that naked stuff isn't good for my joints in the cold weather."

"I agree with you there. Well, let's get it over and done with. Can you two birds fly ahead, please? Tell The Fern we're on our way. Come along. I'll let you drive. You know my directions aren't good in that part of the forest."

They picked up their bags and climbed into the little 2CV. Agnes put a spell on the cottage to keep intruders out, and they set off.

Some time later they arrived at the middle of the forest. Not exactly the middle, but as close as they could get without angering The Fern. Man-made objects weren't tolerated by

The Fern, which was why they had to undress and tramp the last mile or so naked.

"This isn't good for my feet or for my joints either," complained Doris.

"Same here," replied Agnes." She sighed. "But the Fern's rules are not to be broken. I hope it isn't something arduous or complicated."

"She's only given us simple tasks since we got old."

"Yes, but if it's simple, why the urgency?"

"Hmm. Good question. Do you have a good answer?"

"No."

"Thought you might say that."

They carried on in silence, apart from the occasional greeting to a bird or squirrel. They reached the centre of the forest where they sat on tree stumps and waited. They didn't see The Fern. That's how she was. She was the oldest living thing on the planet and liked her privacy. Suddenly her booming voice seemed to come out of nowhere. Or everywhere, depending on which way you were facing. They listened and nodded and when everything was silent decided that was the end of the audience.

"I think we're dismissed," Agnes said in a whisper. Doris nodded.

"Yes, I think you're right. Dismissed. Let's get back to the car."

They walked back in silence, not discussing the task, as they didn't know who or what might be listening. Back at the car they dressed and drove back to the cottage. As they parked up Agnes grinned.

"Oh. At least she's filled us up with petrol," said Agnes.

"She did that last time. I don't know how she does that, but I'm not complaining. That's one potion I'll not have to do this week. It's a difficult one."

They had some herbal tea and biscuits and relaxed by the fire before starting to prepare their evening meal. Agnes made some notes while Doris did the cooking. "If I don't do it now, we'll end up forgetting something and we don't want to do that."

"No, we don't want to do that."

## Chapter 2

Molly woke up in hospital. She tried to move, then thought better of it. Her arms and legs were aching, and she had a thumping headache. She tried to turn her head but realised she couldn't as she was in a neck brace. She managed to make a noise, not exactly a shout, but not proper words. Leela had been sitting half asleep in a chair, but on hearing sounds pulled her chair over to the bed and took Molly's hand. She looked into her eyes and smiled.

"Hello, Aunty Molly," she said. "I'm glad you've decided to join us. No, don't try to move, they're waiting for the results of some scan or other to see what's broken and what isn't. They're very nice here. They keep bringing me biscuits and tea, with a bit of help." She winked. Molly tried to wink back but it hurt too much. "Apparently you had a bit of an accident – drove your bike into a Mercedes on the bend near the nature reserve. I don't know what the other chap's like, but the police tell me your bike and his car are pretty much dead. What's the expression he used? Written off. Whatever that means." A tear developed in Molly's eye but didn't run down her cheek because she was laid flat. "Can you think? Will I be able to hear you if you think hard enough?"

'Yes,' came into Leela's head. 'Thank-you for being here. Can you stay until I get the scan results?'

Leela nodded. "Yes, of course I can. I'll straighten things out at work when I go back next week. They'll sign whatever forms I put in front of them to make sure I get paid. I'll be here as long as you need me." Molly tried to smile but winced at the pain. Just then there was a knock at the door and a doctor came in.

"Hello, Miss Grover. Pleased to see you've come round. I have the results of your scan here, and it all looks pretty promising. No broken bones! And no internal injuries either! It really is a miracle how you came through more or less in tact. The paramedics said it must have been a very high speed crash, considering the damage to the vehicles. You'll be in considerable discomfort for some time, but that's just because of the impact. We can start to remove the metalwork and bandages, and we are confident you'll make pretty much a full recovery, but we want to keep you in for a little while to check for concussion. I appreciate you can't ask any questions at the moment, but I'll come back when you're out of all this and we'll have a chat about it. Okay?"

"She wants to know if the police got the other chap," said Leela quickly before the doctor could get away.

"How do you know that?" he asked. "I suppose that's a common question in the circumstances. Yes, the police will be interviewing him as soon as he comes round. He's in worse condition than you, so it might be a few days before that can happen. They'll want to talk to you too, when you're up to it."

"I'll stay here with her," said Leela.

"No, you can go home and come back tomorrow." She tugged at his sleeve and stared hard into his eyes. He looked a bit vague for a moment. "Yes, of course you can stay." He turned and left the room, rubbing his forehead, wondering what had just happened. Leela grinned.

'Well done, girl. You're a chip off the old block,' came the thought into Leela's head. She grinned again and patted Molly's hand. She sat back in the chair and waited. They didn't have to wait too long; a nurse and a doctor came in and carefully removed all the bandages and splints and braces, then rebandaged some parts.

"You can sit up if you want to, now," the doctor said. Molly nodded and smiled, and they slowly raised the top of the bed to about forty-five degrees.

"Thank-you," she said. "That's much better. I can see my dear Leela properly now. Can I have something to eat and drink?"

"Of course," answered the doctor. "We'll sort something out. It's a while to dinner." The nurse went out and a few minutes later a volunteer came in with tea and toast and biscuits. As Leela took the tray she stared hard at the volunteer, who came back a few minutes later with tea and toast for Leela.

After they had all gone Molly burst into tears. Leela tried to console her but putting an arm around her shoulders caused her pain, so Leela just held her hand.

"My Arnold! My poor Arnold!" Molly sobbed. "That monster killed him!"

"Arnold?" queried Leela.

"Arnold, my bike. If he's a write-off, that's as good as saying he's dead!"

"Try not to upset yourself, Aunty Molly," Leela whispered. "As soon as you're well enough you'll have your revenge on him. I'll see to that. We'll do it together."

"You are a good child. I know I can rely on you. We'll do it together, as soon as I am well enough."

## Chapter 3

Theresa took a deep breath and walked into the office building. This was the first time she'd had a job that didn't involve working for Daddy. The people had seemed really nice at all three interviews, but she got the impression they expected her to produce results pretty quickly. Still, she was looking forward to the new challenge, so best foot forward. She approached the reception desk and smiled.

"I'm Theresa Wheatley. I'm starting work here today."

"Ah, yes," said the receptionist. "Have a seat. I'll let Kirsty know you're here. Would you like a coffee or tea?"

"Oh, coffee, please. White, no sugar." She sat down and made sure her clothes and hair were straight while she waited for the coffee. The receptionist returned with a tray bearing two cups and a few biscuits.

"Come this way, please. Kirsty is waiting for you."

She got up and followed the receptionist, almost forgetting her briefcase, but recovering it before anyone had a chance to notice and was led into the lift which took them to the top floor. Kirsty's office was light and spacious, overlooking the car park. The receptionist placed the tray on a small table in a corner near the window. Kirsty smiled and they shook hands and sat at the table.

"No need to be scared," Kirsty laughed. "We're all friendly here. By the time you've been here a few weeks you'll think you've known us all your life."

"Sorry. Does it show that much?"

Kirsty nodded and giggled. "Policy here is to employ people that will fit in. I'm sure you will, as does Ivan, or we wouldn't have hired you. Don't worry. You'll spend your first week with me getting to know everyone, getting to understand how the company works, what our main products and customers are, where the coffee machines and toilets are, important things like that. Then I'll pass you over to Ivan and the real work begins."

Theresa seemed a bit more relaxed. "Sounds good. The reason I'm a bit nervous is that in my last two jobs, that is, in all my jobs since finishing uni, I've worked for my father. This is the first job I've had without him, and I'm not sure what to expect. Not that it will affect my work, of course. I always do my best."

"Of course. You wouldn't have an academic record like yours without doing your best. But let's put that aside for now. Basic facts. Your immediate manager is Ivan. He's Technical Director and head of product development and production. I'm Managing Director, and in charge of just about everything else, admin, finance, HR, marketing, but Wayne, the Sales Director, he has considerable input into marketing. You'll meet him this afternoon. He's nice. Everyone's nice here. Oh, and by the way, Ivan is also my husband. Just give a shout when you want more coffee. Let's get down to business. There'll be time to chat later. I've arranged for sandwiches in the conference room for lunch, for an informal opportunity to meet Wayne and one or two other senior people. I hope that's okay?"

"Yes, of course. I was wondering about lunch; I don't know this part of town and need to find out where to eat and where not to eat." They both had a giggle at that.

"Good. Here's a file about the company, policies, rules, forms, you know, things you'll need to know. Let's go through it together until we need a break." She produced a lever arch file and they started ploughing through it.

Lunch time came and they walked along to the conference room which was at the other end of the top floor. Theresa was used to soaking up information, but she was relieved to have a break as there was a lot to take in. None of it complicated, but an awful lot. Another five people joined them and they selected their food from trays of sandwiches, savoury items, cakes, etc, and sat around one end of the table. When they all had drinks, Kirsty addressed them.

"You all know who Theresa is, but she doesn't know who does what. Let's say a few words about ourselves, what we do, which department, interesting hobbies, stuff like that." Wayne, Zoe, Robson and Carl introduced themselves. She had already met Ivan at the interview stage. "Right," said Kirsty when they had all spoken. "Now your turn. Tell us about yourself and your previous jobs."

"Well, I'm married to Barry who works at the local factory, I have a degree in Chemistry from Cambridge, and in my last job I worked at the university as Technical Assistant to my father, Professor Watson, and before that I worked for him in his own consultancy before he took up the post at the university."

"What sort of things did he do?" asked Wayne.

"He was professor of psychic research, but he has just retired. Telepathy, psychokinesis, seeing the future, things like that. My work involved looking after the technology used to detect radio waves, thought processes, ultrasound, etc. Very interesting."

"I bet it was," Wayne responded. "I'd like to hear more about it." Kirsty and Ivan had been giving each other knowing looks while she was talking.

"So would I, but not right now," Kirsty butted in. They chatted a bit more until Kirsty announced that lunch was over. As the others left, she asked Ivan to stay behind.

"Theresa, I'm going to show you something, which is our personal secret. No-one here knows about it other than Ivan and me. But first I must insist that you don't mention it to any other employee here, or anyone outside the company either. One or two might suspect, but only Ivan knows for certain. Do you give me your word?"

"Yes, of course. Confidentiality was an essential part of my work at the uni. It goes without saying in this sort of environment too, I would imagine."

"Good. Thank-you." She pointed at a slice of cake on a plate in the middle of the table. "Watch carefully." The slice fell over. "Is that the sort of thing your father worked on?"

"Oh, yes!" said Theresa, obviously delighted.

"You don't seem surprised," said Ivan.

"Well, no. That's the sort of thing he investigated. My part was to make sure it was genuine, that there weren't any wires or magnetic fields or anything to make it happen when it wasn't real." Kirsty and Ivan looked at one another.

"So that was an every-day occurrence?" asked Ivan.

"Not every-day, but frequent, certainly."

"It isn't something we do in our line of business. I just thought you might be interested," said Kirsty.

"And not scared," added Ivan.

"Scared? No! Why would I be scared?"

"No reason," said Kirsty. "It's just that we know someone who can do it better than I can, and I'm not on good terms with her, so if I upset her, she might want to take revenge."

"Oh, I see. That could be scary. But let's hope it doesn't get to that, eh?"

"Exactly. Now, back to work, and not a word. I wouldn't have mentioned it if it hadn't been for your previous job. Just in case we need you in an emergency."

"Oh, but I can't do it."

"No, but you understand how it can happen, and wouldn't assume you were imagining it."

"Right. I'll stay mum but be on my guard."

"That's the ticket." Ivan got up and left. "Right. We'll leave the employee manual for today. Let's meet some people and see the products."

## Chapter 4

Doris and Agnes tucked into their bowls of soup and considered the task ahead.

"It's alright her saying there's a rogue witch about then not telling us who it is," said Doris.

"Yes, but perhaps she doesn't know," replied Agnes.

"Doesn't know? But she's supposed to know everything. Doesn't know, my foot!"

"Or perhaps she isn't telling us to keep us on our toes. And she does think there's more than one. That's why we have to keep it to ourselves and not involve other witches."

"You could have a point there. She definitely told us not to trust others and make the team up from ordinary people."

"Well, I don't trust Molly, for a start. Never have done, never will. But I don't really know many others I wouldn't trust."

"You've got to admit there are some we don't know well enough to trust or not trust. Alice, for instance. She seems perfectly nice, but we know nothing about her. I've only met her once."

"Yes. You're right. Anyway, who are we going to include in our team?"

"Haven't a clue. Try to think of someone really clever." There was a long silence.

"Can't think of any."

"Nor can I." Another long pause.

"Just a minute. What about that clever girl from the Frobisher Project? You know, the Beech Tree Forest Camp. They were all bright children, but if you go back about fifteen years or so there was one particularly bright girl. Kirsty I think her name might have been."

"I'm not sure who you mean. The one with the blonde ringlets who spoke three languages?"

"No. Not that one. The little one with the dark hair. Went out of her way to comfort the bullying victims."

"Ah, yes! I think I know the one. Was her name Kirsty?"

"Just a minute. I'll go back and see if I can find her." Agnes put her spoon down, wiped her mouth, closed her eyes and went into a trance. Ten minutes later she opened her eyes and took a drink from her tumbler. "Yes, Kirsty. I found a few of them: Ivan, Stacey, Zoe. Leela was the trouble maker. Do you remember, the one who wasn't there when we went back? And the place had an aroma of Molly. I think they were related."

"Yes, that's right. I remember now. I bet Leela is one we can't trust."

"I'll do another trance and try to find out where she is and if she is going to be useful. You decide what we need to take." Agnes repeated the process and remained motionless for about an hour. When she came back, she was worn out and Doris fussed over her, giving her herbal biscuits and drinks. After ten minutes she was back to normal. Doris had assembled her personal 'toolkit' of potions in little aerosol bottles, powders in plastic boxes with clip-on lids, various twigs and leaves in paper bags, and a selection of biscuits and drinks to keep them going on the journey.

"Okay, what have you found?"

"She's married to Ivan, one of the other bright kids. They work in a successful company in an industrial park not far from the town centre, doing electronic stuff, so they are obviously still on the bright side of normal. It is in …"

"Come on, come on, where is it?"

"Oh, be patient!" She closed her eyes again, but only briefly this time. "It is in Thorsley, which isn't far from here."

"Good. I'll leave the driving to you. You're less likely to get lost. Come on."

"No! Wait a bit. I need a rest after all that!"

"Of course. Sorry. I've got what I need. Is there anything of yours I can put together while you're resting?"

"Just the usual stuff. A wand or two, my special mirror, all three compasses, my box of lenses and magnifying glasses, and anything else you think might be useful. Remember we don't know what we're going to do or what we might find until we get there."

"And we don't know who we'll be up against either. The Fern said not to trust any witches. We've identified Molly and her niece, Leela, so far, and possibly Alice, but no-one else."

"Does Leela count as a witch?"

"Not sure, but she *is* Molly's niece so I would imagine she has been trained up by now. There was an air of wickedness about her from the start." Doris rummaged around in Agnes' corner of the workshop and managed to find everything on the list. She also added a few things she saw on the desk, such as some magic pebbles and some feathers, and put them into Agnes' favourite bag. She put these on the back seat of the car, making sure she could reach them from the front seat if need be, and went to check on Agnes, who was now sitting up.

"I'm feeling much refreshed now. Are we ready to set off? What have you got in my bag?" They discussed the equipment Doris had assembled, and Agnes seemed satisfied with Doris' work. "Right. Let's go. If I feel a bit wavy you might have to take over the driving, but I'll do the difficult bits." So saying they got into the car. Agnes opened the window to give instructions to a few small animals and birds, put a spell on the house to keep intruders out, and away they went.

## Chapter 5

The little 2CV pulled into the car park and they got out, with their bags. The journey had taken less than an hour, and Agnes had managed to drive the entire journey, much to the relief of Doris, who drove as little as possible. The two sisters didn't have anything that could be described as 'business attire' but they had put on their best dresses and cardigans to create a good impression. Doris had her bag at the ready with a few potions in easy reach. They went in and walked up to the reception desk in as business-like a fashion as they could manage. Doris sprayed a little mist from a bottle into the air and flapped an arm to spread it about.

"Good afternoon," Agnes said to the receptionist, once the potion had had time to take effect. "We are Miss Swales and Miss Swales, and we're here to see Kirsty."

"Is she expecting you?" the receptionist asked, looking down a list of visitors. "I can't see your names on the list. Which company are you from?"

Agnes was taken aback at this, but while the woman was distracted Doris gave her another spray. "We're from The Fern," Doris said, "and she might not be actually expecting us, but she won't be surprised. She'll know us as soon as she sees us."

The receptionist picked up the phone and explained to Kirsty. Kirsty wasn't in the mood for random visitors, as she had lots of work to do with short deadlines, but she agreed to come down. When she emerged from the lift Doris gave another spray, and Kirsty's frown immediately became a smile. "Good afternoon, Miss Swales and Miss Swales. Please come up to my office. She guided them into the lift and up they went. "I know you from somewhere, don't I?" she asked as she seated them.

They nodded. "Yes, from the Godfrey Frobisher Project at Beech Tree Forest Camp quite a few years ago now," said Agnes. "But please feel free to call us Agnes and Doris, now that you're grown up." Doris kept giving a little spray of her potion every now and again, to keep Kirsty amenable.

"Yes, of course, I remember now," Kirsty replied. "So what brings you here? What can I do for you?"

"It's difficult to explain," said Agnes.

"Yes, difficult," echoed Doris.

"You see, we need you to help us solve a problem, but at the moment we aren't certain what the problem is."

"You're not making sense and my time is precious. I must ask you to leave," Kirsty remonstrated.

"Quick, more spray," Agnes hissed at Doris, who quickly pulled a different aerosol from her bag and sprayed Kirsty liberally with it.

Kirsty tried to waft it away at first, but then smiled. "I'm sorry, please go on."

"There will be an attempt at a crime, and we've been instructed to prevent it. We don't know what it is, or when the attempt will be made, but do you remember Leela?"

Kirsty shuddered. "Yes, Leela, the school bully. Did what she wanted and always got away with it. I know how she did it, but when I tried, it didn't seem to work."

"Yes. That sounds like her family," said Doris. "We need to put a team together to confound her plotting."

"That sounds a bit melodramatic, dear," said Agnes. She turned back to Kirsty. "But that's about it. Leela, or someone close to her, perhaps her Aunt Molly, is plotting a crime of some sort, and it's up to us to stop it. We've been told not to use our people because we don't know how many we can trust, so we're looking to involve highly intelligent young people, like yourself, to stop the carnage."

"Now who's being melodramatic? Yes, to stop the carnage. You will help us. Who else do you know who is highly intelligent and reliable?"

"Well, I don't know what to say," said Kirsty, looking confused. "I want to refuse to take part, but somehow I can't. There's my husband, Ivan, and a handful of my closest colleagues, Wayne, Robson, Carl, Zoe, they were all on the Frobisher project, and Theresa the new woman."

"Right," said Agnes in a very business-like manner. "Let's get them in and we'll get them on board."

Just then there was a knock at the door and a young woman popped in. "Sorry to interrupt, but don't forget you have a meeting with Mr Hammond in ten minutes. He's just phoned to say he's just got off the train and he's looking for a taxi."

Agnes slipped a white pebble into Kirsty's hand and closed her fingers round it, holding her hand tightly.

"Oh, can you cancel him?"

"No. He's on his way, bang on time as usual. He'll be here in less than five minutes."

"When he arrives, show him into a little room and I'll have a word with him," said Doris with a smile."

The woman looked uncertainly to Kirsty for confirmation, who nodded. Mr Hammond arrived and was shown to a room. Doris followed him in and asked him to sit down. She sprayed the room with one of her potions then slipped something into his hand. It was a small twig, about four inches long, with small round leaves along its length.

She closed his fingers around it and gave the room another spray for good measure.

"Kirsty will be along soon. Don't worry. It isn't her fault you're much too early." She smiled at him, and he smiled back.

"Yes, of course, much too early," he muttered, clutching the twig as she left the room.

Back in Kirsty's office the people she mentioned had assembled. Some were anxious to get away as they had been pulled from important work or meetings. Doris crept in behind them, giving the room a spray as she walked along the line to her seat. Agnes explained the situation and asked for their help. They all seemed flustered at first, but eventually, all agreed to help. "Good," said Agnes. "We'll come back when we have more to tell you. Now don't forget, not a word to anyone. If the 'others' know we're on to them, well, it could be curtains for the lot of us." She shook hands with them all, followed by Doris who gave each one a twig as she shook their hands.

"Keep this on you at all times. It will help in ways you cannot imagine," Doris told them, and the sisters left. The people mulled about in Kirsty's office, confused, and went back to work.

"Well," said Kirsty to herself. "What was that all about? And where did this pebble come from? I don't know what came over me." The woman came back in and reminded her about Mr Hammond. "Oh, the poor man! I've kept him waiting for almost an hour!" she said, glancing at her watch and rushing out. In the little office Mr Hammond was sitting smiling happily and clutching the twig. "Mr Hammond, I'm so sorry for delaying you. Please come along to my office."

"Oh, no," he replied, looking a bit confused. "No need to apologise. It's my fault for arriving too early. Much, much too early."

## Chapter 6

The police officer stood at the foot of the bed. Molly slurped her tea and eyed him suspiciously.

"I'm sorry to visit you so soon, Mrs Grover," he began.

"It's 'Miss', actually," interjected Leela.

"Sorry, Miss Grover," he apologised while he altered his notes. "As I was saying, I'm sorry to visit you so soon, but we generally find that people's memories are more accurate that way. If we waited a few days your memory might become clouded."

"Clouded?" said Molly. "He thinks because I'm old I'm losing my marbles!"

"Oh, no, not at all. This applies to people of all ages. The fact that you can ride a motorcycle implies that you have your marbles, if you want to put it that way."

"Okay, you're forgiven."

"Thank-you. Now then, on the day of the accident you were going towards the town centre when you crossed onto the wrong side of the road."

"Now just a minute," Molly said indignantly. "Who says I was on the wrong side of the road?"

The officer was taken aback. "The report from the accident investigation officer says that your tyre tracks were on the wrong side of the road."

"Well, I wasn't. I was on the correct side, and the idiot in the Merc came screaming round the corner on the wrong side and ran straight into me."

"I'm sorry. I'll have that checked, but the report from the investigating officer says he was on the correct side, and you were on the wrong side."

"Young man, come closer and sit down."

"I'd rather stand," he said, moving closer.

"I said sit down. Do it now." He sat in the chair Leela had vacated. "Take my hand and look into my eyes." He did as instructed. "I was on the correct side of the road," she said slowly and firmly while staring hard into his eyes.

"You were on the correct side of the road," he repeated slowly. "That's obvious. There's no doubt about that fact." She released his hand. He altered his notes then stood up and rubbed his eyes. "Thank-you, Miss Grover. I think that's all for now. I might need to come back to ask you further questions, perhaps tomorrow or later in the week." He turned to leave and shook his head as he left, feeling confused and not sure which way to go in the corridor.

He went along to another ward to visit the car driver.

"I'm sorry," said the nurse. "Mr Blomberg is still unconscious. You won't be able to interview him today."

"Okay, thanks." He gave her a card with his details. "Please let us know as soon as we can talk to him."

She took the card and read it with a smile. "Will do. It certainly won't be today. Perhaps tomorrow, Troy." He smiled back at her and left.

Back in his car he read through his notes. "I don't understand this. According to these notes they were on different sides of the road. How did they collide?" he muttered to himself.

He returned to the police station and wrote up his notes.

"I'm puzzled, sarge," he said. "This report says Miss Grover was on the wrong side of the road, but I know for a fact she wasn't."

The sergeant read through what was on the screen. "They collided, so they must have been on the same side," he said, trying not to sound sarcastic, as the young officer was generally very thorough. "What makes you think they weren't?"

"Miss Grover said she was on the correct side."

"The accident officer says she wasn't."

"I know that, sarge, but I know Miss Grover is right, so the accident officer must be mistaken."

"I'll have a quiet word with him. This guy doesn't usually make mistakes. Have you interviewed the other driver yet?"

"No, sarge. He's still unconscious."

"Okay. See what he says when he comes round. I'm assuming he will come round?"

"Yes, sarge. The doctors are pretty confident he will."

"Because if he doesn't, this could be murder, or manslaughter at the very least."

"Yes, sarge, but Miss Grover was on the correct side of the road, so it could be suicide, couldn't it?"

"That depends on the accident investigation team. I'll have a word with them later today."

"Yes, sarge."

"What makes you think the lady was on the correct side?"

"She said she was."

"When you question criminals, do they always tell the truth?"

"No, sarge."

"But Miss Grover always does?"

"Yes sarge."

"No doubt about it?"

"None whatsoever, sarge. She told me so herself."

"Tell me, is Miss Grover young and attractive?"

"No, sarge. She's about seventy and not at all, er, well, she looks like you might expect a seventy-year-old woman to look. Shall we say I didn't find her attractive, but other people might?"

"Good answer." A young female officer at the next desk tried to supress a giggle.

## Chapter 7

A few days later Molly was discharged from hospital. The doctors decided she didn't have concussion, and no broken bones. Her cuts and grazes were bandaged up and Leela was given spare bandages, ointment, and instructions on how to change them and how often. She moved in with Molly to help with meals and bandages, visiting her own flat every day or so just to keep an eye on it. A week later they got a visit from a police officer. Not the one who had visited the hospital, but a different one, older and more business-like.

"I'm sorry, Mrs Grover," he began.

"It's Miss Grover. I told the other policeman that. Are you all stupid?" Leela said aggressively.

"No need for that, dear," Molly said to Leela, quite harshly. She turned to the officer. "Please excuse my niece," she apologised. "She's at an age, you know. I'm sure you'll understand if you have teenage daughters," she said with a smile and a wink.

"I'm not a teenager!" Leela growled.

"Well, stop behaving like one, then," Molly remarked. Leela sat down, scowling, and folded her arms firmly.

"Don't worry, miss," the officer said with a smile. "We experience all sorts in the force. Anyway, the reason I'm here today is to check a few facts about your accident, if you don't mind."

"No, quite alright. Go ahead."

"Well, you say you were on the correct side of the road."

"Correct."

"But the other driver insists you weren't."

"Well he's obviously wrong. He probably had a bump on the head and can't remember properly."

"And the accident investigation team say your tyre marks tell them you were on the wrong side of the road too."

"They must be mistaken."

"And the photographs they took support what they say."

"It can't be possible. I was on the right side – the left, that is – and he drove into me. I don't know what he was thinking at the time. I couldn't read his mind."

"No, we don't usually rely on mind reading for forensic evidence. But on the evidence we have I'm obliged to place you under arrest for dangerous driving, driving in a manner likely to cause serious injury or death. In view of your age and the fact that you still haven't recovered from your injuries I am not taking you in for further investigation at the moment, but when this comes to court, we may want to have you medically examined, but that isn't my decision. Thank-you for your co-operation, Miss Grover. I'll see myself out." He turned and left.

Molly and Leela sat in stunned silence for a moment, then Molly called out. "Don't let him get away! I haven't been into his mind yet!" Leela rushed to the door, but she was too late. His car disappeared round the corner.

"Damn!" exclaimed Leela. "Damn! Damn! Damn! I'm not going to let this rest. I'll be avenged on them all." She pulled on a jacket and left the house, getting into her car and heading for the town centre.

Molly closed her eyes and concentrated for a while. "It's no good; she's blocked me, just like that idiot in the Merc did. I hope she doesn't do anything stupid. She can be very hot headed, just like her idiot father," she mumbled to herself. "She doesn't get it from our side of the family."

In the town centre Leela found a parking place. She got out of the little car, slammed the door, and locked it. She stomped her way to the town square and stood in the middle, hands on hips, and glared at the passing shoppers. Soon she saw what she had come for – a police officer going about his duty. She approached him, and he smiled, asking how he could help. She glared at him, pointed an out-stretched arm at him, and he fell to the floor, dead. She stormed off while a group of shoppers gathered round. One telephoned the police, another telephoned for an ambulance, but there was nothing anyone could do. Minutes later it happened again in another part of the town centre, just twenty or so yards away. Within ten minutes there were about fifteen police officers in riot gear looking for her. After she had killed another three, they were ordered to withdraw but find places where they could keep an eye on her.

Back at the central police station heads were being scratched. Five officers dead, without explanation, with no signs of injury or trauma, and no member of the public hurt in any way, other than the shock of seeing it happen. The senior officer at the station was on the phone to those higher up asking for help and advice, suggesting support from the army, but wasn't really making himself understood. People at the county HQ were asking each other if he had been drinking, but he assured them not. They sent a team of plain-clothed specialists to assess the bodies and another team to survey the town centre. Those assessing the bodies were soon joined by paramedics who took the dead officers away to the mortuary at the local hospital. The other team spread out, and it didn't take long for one of them to spot Leela. He emerged from behind a bus shelter and shouted to her,

"Police officer with a Taser. Police officer with a Taser. Drop your weapon and put your hands in the air. Drop your weapon now and put your hands in the air. Do as I say. Do it now!"

She laughed at him. "Weapon? What weapon?" She put her hands up, then lowered her right arm to point at the officer, and he fell to the ground, dead. The other officers had been watching this and all made sure they were out of her line of sight.

## Chapter 8

Doris was just finishing washing the breakfast dishes when she heard a scratching sound at the door. She opened it, and there stood a small fox. "Hello, darling," she said, scratching the top of its head. The fox began to cough, and eventually coughed up a small green package, which Doris picked up and carefully unwrapped. She read the message on it, then called for her sister. "Agnes! Agnes! Come quick! Message from The Fern! She says it's started and we have to go now!" She gave the fox a couple of herbal biscuits which he ate ravenously. Agnes came bustling through, pulling on her cardigan as she came. "Are you okay?" Doris asked the fox. He nodded. "Good. Please go back to The Fern and tell her we're on our way." The fox nodded again, turned round, and disappeared into the undergrowth. The sisters grabbed their bags from behind the door, in which they had their toolkits ready, expecting the call any day, and climbed into the little car. Agnes did her usual securing of the cottage and away they went.

They weren't really sure where they were going, but whenever there was any doubt Agnes let go of the wheel and let the car decide. The car took them to the car park behind the electronics firm, where Kirsty saw them out of her office window. "Oh, dear," she said. She picked up the phone and called Ivan. "They're here. I suppose that means it is starting, whatever it is."

"Yes, you're probably right. I'll get the others and assemble in your office. It's strange. I don't want to do this, but I can't stop myself."

"Me too, but there we go," Kirsty replied. She took the lift down to reception and greeted the sisters as they came in.

"Let's go up to my office," she said, and they followed her into the lift, Doris giving a quick spray, just in case. When they got there the others had arrived and sat round the table.

"Our task has begun," said Agnes without waiting. "We don't know what it is, but we've been sent to the town centre, so you must come with us, bringing whatever you think we might need."

"As we don't know what we are about to do, perhaps two of us should go with you, then the rest can follow when we know what's what," said Kirsty.

"Good idea," said Doris. "Who is coming with us?"

"I'll go," volunteered Wayne. "I've got a parking pass for town, and I'm probably the strongest here."

"Thanks, Wayne," said Kirsty. "Zoe, do you want to go too? You know your way around the centre better than most."

"Okay," answered Zoe. "Shall we be off then? As it's urgent."

"Good," said Agnes. "Let's go." She hurried to the lift followed by the others. Downstairs they got into Wayne's car, which was considerably bigger and more comfortable than the sisters' car. Before they got there Zoe's phone rang. It was Kirsty, telling them that there had been some sort of killing of police officers in the town square. "I say," said Agnes. "That's a clever little thing. We'll have to get one."

"What, my phone?" said Zoe, perplexed.

"Yes. Never seen anything like that before." Zoe and Wayne glanced at each other, trying not to laugh. Wayne parked up behind some shops and they got out.

"Best be quiet," he whispered. "We don't know what we're going to find." They made their way along an alleyway and stopped just before the end, which emerged onto the high street between two big shops. They could see Leela wandering about killing every police officer she saw. They watched for a few minutes then went back along the alleyway. "I've got the gist of what's going on," said Wayne.

"So have I," said Zoe. "But what can we do about it?"

"Let's go back to the office," he whispered. On the way you can tell Kirsty what we saw. She and Ivan might come up with some ideas. We need a way to stop Leela. It would help if we could get a better view without putting ourselves at risk."

"Yes. The surveillance room at the police station would be a good start. My brother helped instal the camera system. They can see every part of the town centre."

"Off you go then, and tell the others," said Doris. "I'll stay here and help where I can." Wayne and Zoe glanced at one another, confused but Agnes chivvied them back to the car.

"She knows what she's doing. Come on," said Agnes.

Back at the office they considered the problem. "If she can kill at will it's going to be difficult to stop her," said Ivan after a great deal of discussion.

"Here's a thought," said Theresa. "You know the AI generator that tracks movement and predicts behaviour?"

"Of course I know it," said Ivan. "I designed it and built the prototype."

"Well," Theresa said slowly. "Could we reverse the polarity on the sensors and feed that into the force field generator to create a negative force field?"

"I see what you mean," said Ivan after a moment of thought. "Use the force field to keep things in rather than keep them out."

"Exactly," said Theresa. "Then if we can attach it to her somehow, she won't be able to escape, and anything she tries to throw won't leave her. I don't know what it is she's throwing, but it's the best I can come up with."

"Right. It's the only idea we've got for now, so let's give it a go. Good thinking, Theresa. Come to my office and we'll try to design it. Meanwhile, is there any way of getting into the surveillance room at the police station? I imagine they won't let random people in, but if we did get in we could reroute one of their computers to our main system to see what's happening."

"I could get one of you inside," piped up Agnes, much to everyone's amazement. They stared at her, waiting for an explanation. "You're all agreeing to do this, even though you don't want to, aren't you?" They looked at each other and nodded. "Well, this is very much the same, but taking it a bit further."

"I suppose so," said Kirsty. "Carl, you're our top computer man. Can you do it?"

"Yes, that's the easy bit," he replied. "It's getting in and persuading them to let me fiddle with their computers that's difficult."

"Piece of cake, young man," said Agnes. "Come on, get what kit you need and let's be off." She picked up her bag and headed for the lift. Carl shrugged his shoulders and followed her.

## Chapter 9

In Ivan's office he and Theresa started drawing circuit diagrams on the whiteboard, when Zoe, Robson and Wayne came in. "Anything we can do?" asked Robson.

"There will be in about ten minutes," said Ivan. "We'll need a solar power pack about the size of a small matchbox to give enough juice for the AI generator and force field generator to keep them both going for a couple of hours from a single charge. Can you and Zoe do that? It has to be light enough to stick to her skin with superglue, and not come off. We're about to make it. Theresa will wire up the board and I'll program the chip."

"Okay. We're onto it," said Zoe. They left the room and headed for the workshop.

"What about me?" asked Wayne. "I know I don't have the technical skills of you techy folk, but I want to be useful."

"Don't worry, mate," Ivan grinned. "We want your muscles." Wayne looked puzzled. "We want you to be the guineapig. We'll test it on you."

"Should have kept my mouth shut," said Wayne with a wry grin.

"Don't worry. We won't hurt you. You're the biggest and strongest of all of us. That's why we need to test it on you."

Twenty minutes later they had a little device in their hands. "Right, Wayne, take your shirt off and turn round," Ivan told him. "We won't stick it on with superglue, just a bit of transparent tape for now. Stick it on him, Robson." Wayne winced as the eight barbed needles dug into his flesh, but the pain was momentary. Ivan took some tissues for a box and rolled them into balls, then passed them to Wayne. He also gave him a few heavier items, such as a stapler, a pencil sharpener and a hole-punch from his desk. "Stand back. I'm going to turn it on." Ivan pressed a few keys on his laptop and looked up. "Are you okay, Wayne?" he asked. Wayne nodded stiffly. "Okay. Try to throw the tissue balls." Wayne obviously had restricted movement in his arms, but he managed to throw a tissue ball, which only travelled a few inches before dropping to the floor at his feet. He tried throwing the stapler, with the same outcome "Good," said Ivan. "Can you walk?" Wayne took a few slow cumbersome steps forward.

"Yes," he replied. "I can walk, but it's like wading through treacle."

"Hmm. Not good enough. I'm going to up the power a bit. Okay?"

"Do I have a choice?"

"No." Ivan did some more key pressing. "How's that?"

"I can't move at all, and I'm struggling to talk," Wayne muttered through gritted teeth."

"But you can breathe okay?"

"Yes, but it's a struggle."

"Can you throw anything?"

"No. Can't move my arm enough for that."

"Good. I'm going to turn it off now. Be ready to support him." Ivan pressed more keys and Wayne almost collapsed but was caught by the others. "I'd call that a success. If it can stop the mighty Wayne, I'm sure it can stop Leela. Let's get it charged up. Put it under a few bright lights, Robson. Do you think it will be fully charged in ten minutes?"

"Should be," answered Robson. "I'll give it a go." He took the device back to the workshop. Ten minutes later he was ready, and Robson, Zoe, Wayne and Ivan gathered in reception. On the way to the town square, they discussed their action plan.

## Chapter 10

In town Doris was following Leela around and forcing a few drops of liquid into the mouths of each of Leela's victims, bringing them round a few moments later. The officers in the square couldn't see her. They radioed in to the station. "New development. She's still going round killing people, but they get up a short while later. They look a bit out of it, as though they've had too much to drink, but at least they're alive."

"It's that old lady. She's giving them something."

"What old lady? Don't know what you're talking about."

"There's an old lady following her around and putting something into their mouths to revive them."

"Can't see her."

"Are you blind? She's there, just a few feet from you now!"

"Never mind that. I'm going to have a go with the Taser."

"Remember what happened to Grant and watch out you don't hit the old lady."

"I'm in full body armour – Grant wasn't. And shut up about the old lady. There isn't one!"

The officer stepped forward from behind the advertising hoarding and shouted to Leela. "Police officer with a Taser! Police officer with a Taser! Drop your weapon and put your hands in the air. Drop your weapon now and put your hands in the air. Do as I say. Do it now!"

Leela turned to face him and laughed. She pointed at him, and he fell to the floor, despite his body armour. As soon as she turned away Doris ran out and forced a few drops of liquid into his mouth and he came round immediately. He was groggy and hung onto the hoarding to get to his feet, with the help of a few members of the public.

Meanwhile, Agnes and Carl had arrived at the Police Station. They went in, Agnes spraying as they walked, and asked to be taken to the surveillance room.

"I'm sorry, madam, but you can't go in there," the desk officer replied.

"I don't think you understand," said Agnes, spraying him. "We need to go there urgently."

The man looked confused but agreed to their request and let them in through a side door. Upstairs they were led in, and everyone faced them with hostile expressions until Agnes had given them a good spraying. "Carry on with your work," she instructed them. "Is there a computer we can use?" A young woman pointed to one at an unoccupied desk, and Carl sat down and got to work.

After a few minutes he phoned Kirsty. "Can you see anything?" he asked.

"Good work, mate. I have the town centre on my pc and Wayne's, and we have control of the cameras. We can see Leela killing people and Doris reviving them. Stay there if you need to, but if you can lock the pc, make your way to the town square. The others are on their way there now. They might need your help."

"Okay. It's locked. They would have to take the entire system down to unlock it without my involvement. I'll head for the town and find the others."

"Good. We'll offer them help later. Stay out of sight when you get there."

Carl and Agnes met the others behind a clump of bushes in what the council laughably called a garden while Kirsty directed them to hiding places and kept them up to date with goings on in places they couldn't see. Zoe prepared the device by putting some superglue around the edge. Ivan was ready with his laptop, and on Kirsty's instruction the operation began. Wayne, Carl and Robson ran out onto the town square, shouting and swearing at each other, and pretending to fight. Everyone looked round at them, and two police officers tried to separate them.

"We're only pretending. We're a diversion," Wayne whispered as he dragged the officer to the ground.

Leela also turned to see what was what and laughed when she saw the three apparently drunk men getting the better of the officers. Zoe ran out and slapped the device onto Leela's back between the shoulder blades just above the neckline of her blouse and gave it a good push to make sure the barbs took hold, and she held it long enough for the superglue to set, despite Leela's struggles. Zoe had been a victim of Leela's bullying at school, and now it was payback time. "It's in!" she shouted to Ivan. "Turn it on! Be quick!" Ivan deftly pressed the necessary keys, and Leela froze." Zoe quickly stepped back from her. "Okay, you can stop now!" she called to the pretend fighters, who released their grips on the officers.

Wayne gave his officer a hand up and grinned at him. "Sorry about that," he said. "You need to get a van or something to take her away. She can't move at the moment. Get her locked up before it wears off."

The officer muttered his thanks and radioed the station, who sent a van immediately. It was only a few minutes away, and they picked Leela up and put her in the back of the van.

It was a bit like lifting a perspex cylinder which was quite rigid, but totally invisible.

Ivan had emerged from his hiding place and spoke to the officers. "She can't move, but she can breathe; she won't come to any harm. That little box on her back is keeping her immobile, but it's solar powered, so keep a light on her. If she gets into somewhere dark it would run flat in about two hours, and she'd be set free. Keep the lights on, no matter what, until you discover how best to handle her."

Ivan instructed Carl to release the diversion on the surveillance room computer, and Carl went off with Agnes to do that.

## Chapter 11

Molly decided to take advantage of Leela's absence and struggled out of bed. She put some clothes on and stopped a passing car with the power of her mind and forced them to take her to the hospital. She had already discovered the whereabouts of the car driver before she left, and went straight to his ward, mentally disarming anyone who tried to stop her. She walked through the door and stopped.

"Torsten!" she shouted. "Why am I not surprised to see you!"

"Molly!" he replied. "I'm not surprised to learn you're behind this!"

They both stared unblinkingly at each other and concentrated hard. The shouts brought nurses to the room, but they couldn't get in. It was as though there was an invisible door keeping them out.

In the town centre the group of heroes was making its way back to the office when Doris and Agnes stopped suddenly.

"Can you hear that?" Agnes asked.

"I'm afraid I can," Doris replied. "Quick. We need your car," she said, grabbing Wayne. "Take us that way," she pointed to her left. They ran to the car and the three of them got in.

"Where are we going?" asked Wayne.

"That way."

"But where?"

"Haven't a clue, but it's that way." She continued to point, and Wayne followed her instructions.

"I think we're heading toward the hospital," he said as they left the town centre. At the hospital he stopped on

Doris' command, and they ran in, Doris leading the way and Agnes dealing with anyone who tried to stop them. They ran up three flights of stairs and turned into a ward. They came to an abrupt halt at the door of a side room.

"Molly!" shouted Doris. "So you are in league with Leela."

"What do you think you're up to?" said Agnes.

"Keep away," Molly answered. "This is my business; not yours. This idiot put me in hospital and killed my Arnold."

"No, I didn't!" Torsten replied. "She was on the wrong side of the road and drove into my car."

"That's because he blocked me. I was trying to tell him to get out of the way, but his mind was closed."

"Of course. When I heard you were active in the area, I always closed my mind whenever I went out. I know what you're like. You think you're entitled to do what you want and I'm one of the few who can stop you."

"Wayne," Agnes turned to him, whispering. "We need one of those devices we used on Leela. Can they make another and bring it here?" Wayne went round the corner and phoned the office, relaying Agnes' request. When he came back, he didn't say a word, but smiled and nodded to Agnes.

"Now then, Molly, there's three of us and only one of you. I know Torsten's hurt, and we're old, but we're still strong enough to overpower you."

"I'll get Leela here. She's strong enough to take on all three of you. Then I can get my revenge on this idiot here. He thinks he can mess with me! Well he can't. He's killed my Arnold – now I'm going to kill him."

"The thing is, Molly, Leela can't make it. She's locked up in the police station," said Agnes with a grin.

"What?" Molly gasped. "You cannot be serious! She's strong enough to get out of any prison. They might slow her down, but they'll not stop her."

"I'm afraid not, Molly," said Agnes with a satisfied smile. "You're on your own, dear. Doris and I are just summoning up the energy then you'll join her. Just look at you! You can't even beat Torsten! We know he's clever, but he isn't strong and you're not making any progress against him." They kept Molly occupied with their banter for another half hour, with Torsten's mind giving an extra push every now and again, until Zoe and Ivan arrived with the device. They stayed hidden around the corner and Wayne came back to give them the nod.

"Okay! Here we go! Extra push, Torsten!" shouted Doris, and she and Agnes managed to break down the invisible wall across the doorway. The surge of energy knocked Molly to the floor and Wayne and Zoe burst in behind them. Wayne held Molly down while Zoe slammed the device onto Molly's forehead and held it there until the superglue set. Wayne and Zoe released the squirming Molly, who struggled to get up with her hands still bandaged.

"It's set! Turn it on!" Zoe shouted, and Ivan emerged from his hiding place and pressed the necessary keys on his laptop. Molly froze where she lay. Four police officers, summoned by Kirsty, ran into the room and picked Molly up, in her invisible container, and took her downstairs to the waiting van, and from there to the police station.

## Chapter 12

Wayne took the sisters back to the office while Ivan and Zoe visited the police station to explain the device.

"It's an inverse forcefield," he said to the custody sergeant, showing him the circuit diagrams and the logic programming of the chip. "It's solar powered, so it will last as long as the solar panel does, which should be at least ten years. But you must keep it charged up. Once the power gets below about twenty per cent, she'll be able to break out of it. The same applies to Leela. So keep them in the light at all times. If it goes dark the charge will fall to a dangerous level within about two hours."

The custody sergeant wrote it all down. "Thank-you, Mr Dorranston. I'm not sure I understand all the technical ins and outs, but I understood the bit about the light. We'll do our best to keep them out of mischief, until those upstairs decide what to do next."

"Don't hesitate to contact us if you need any help. I imagine transferring them to a longer term form of custody might be tricky, especially when solicitors get involved. Here's my contact details." He gave them his card and they left.

Back at the office the others were celebrating with tea and cakes. Doris and Agnes arrived back with Wayne and sat down for a rest.

"She's a strong lass, that Molly," said Agnes.

"So was Leela, but we caught Leela by surprise, otherwise we might have had more of a struggle with her." answered Doris. "I'll have to have a sit a while to get myself back together."

"So will I, before that drive home," added Agnes.

"Do you have far to go?" asked Kirsty. "Where do you live? We can take you home, and one of our drivers can deliver the car to you."

"Oh, no, dear," said Agnes. "The car won't be driven by anyone other than us. It's special, you know."

"Yes," added Doris. "And you'd never find our home. It's over that way somewhere." She gestured vaguely with an uncertain hand movement.

"Foxglove Cottage. It's on the edge of the wood. Do you remember when you went to the Frobisher Project at Beech Tree Forest Camp?" Agnes asked. A few of them nodded. "Well, it's nowhere near there."

"Nowhere near there," Doris echoed. They both burst out laughing. The others looked puzzled at first, then they joined in with the laughter.

Ivan documented the technical aspects of the project, with help from Theresa and Zoe, while the others went back to work.

"How do we contact you if we need your help again?" asked Kirsty.

The sisters smiled. "Just think about us, concentrate very hard," said Agnes.

"Yes, very hard," echoed Doris.

"Don't worry, we'll hear you," added Agnes.

## Chapter 13

Leela and Molly had been put into the same cell in the custody suite. That was generally not permitted but considering that neither could move they thought it would save space, as most of the cells were occupied. They could both speak, quietly and with a struggle, but neither could move.

"How are we going to get out of this, Aunty Molly?" asked Leela. Molly tried to shake her head but couldn't manage it.

"I'm going to try something," she said, and closed her eyes. "Did you hear that?" she asked after a moment.

"Yes," Leela answered. "Mushroom soup."

"Good. My thoughts can get through this forcefield, even though my limbs can't. I'm going to try something. Keep quiet for a while." Molly closed her eyes very tightly and concentrated very hard for about an hour. She opened her eyes and smiled. 'Help is on the way in the form of Naomi,' she thought to Leela. Leela smiled and thought a 'thank-you' back to her.

Two hours later there was a flash of light and a tinkling sound. A young woman appeared in the cell, dressed for office work, and with a shimmering light around the edge.

"What's going on here?" she asked. "What have you two got yourselves into?"

'Thanks for coming. I think we need your help. Leela started throwing her weight around and the locals got upset.' Molly thought to her.

'Never mind blaming me!' Leela replied. 'I was taking revenge on your behalf, but the locals were a bit cleverer than we expected. I knew some of them from school. Kirsty and Ivan in particular were terrible swots, and clever to the point of being scary. Ivan in particular.'

"So how are they doing it? What's keeping you in?" She prodded at Molly's cylinder and couldn't break through it.

'Haven't a clue,' Molly thought to her. 'If I knew that we could probably get out ourselves.'

'It's something to do with these little devices. I've got one on my back, and Aunty Molly has one on her forehead.'

Naomi examined the devices the best she could, as she couldn't get close enough to have a really good look. "All I can see is a solar panel, which obviously provides the power, but the business end of it must be inside. Who put these on you?"

'Ivan Dorranston's the brains behind it. I bullied him at school. That was a laugh. What a wimp!' she thought to Naomi.

"But he's got the last laugh. Where can I find Mr Dorranston?"

'Don't know, but it can't be far. He showed up less than an hour after I started my killing spree, and they had the device with them already.'

'And about forty minutes after I locked horns with Torsten,' added Molly.

"Torsten? Torsten Blomberg? I wouldn't have thought he'd be strong enough to cope with you."

'No, normally he wouldn't, but I've been in a road crash, and spent a few days in hospital, then when they let me out nurse Leela here was dosing me up with painkillers and stuff.' Naomi laughed.

'And that's why I was taking revenge for her. The idiot policeman said it was all Aunty Molly's fault, so I was teaching them a lesson.'

"And was it your fault?"

'Well, sort of,' thought Molly. 'I was taking a corner too quickly, as usual, and I put a thought out ahead telling people to get out of the way, but Torsten blocked me, so he never got it and we collided. Totally killed Arnold but made a bit of a mess of his big flash car.'

"I hope you've learned a lesson there. You can't always rely on people listening. You two can both be childish and immature when you want to be. Anyway, I'll seek out this Dorranston chap and work out how to undo it. I'll be back." So saying, she disappeared in a flash of light and tinkling sounds. Fifteen minutes later she was back. "I know where he is. I'm off there now to see what I can find out."

Ivan and Theresa and Zoe were putting the finishing touches to the documentation when there was a flash of light. A young woman appeared in front of them. Theresa's mobile phone started to bleep frantically. She pulled it out of her pocket, glanced at it briefly, and started pressing numbers and letters on it quite urgently. The beeping stopped and Ivan and Zoe fell back into their seats, eyes tight shut and their hands over their ears. There was another flash and the young woman disappeared. Theresa turned the mobile off and they relaxed.

"What was all that about?" asked Zoe, rubbing her ears and blinking.

"That's a little security device I installed on my mobile when I worked for Daddy. I'd forgotten all about it, but it saved us today."

"Saved us? In what way?" asked Ivan.

"That woman was trying to read our minds. When the phone alerted me to it, I was able to turn on a mind blocker. One of my jobs when I worked for Daddy was to detect people who were trying to communicate by telepathy and other forms of thought transference, and the blocker was to stop them when we didn't want them to and permit them at other times. That woman was trying to get the secret of how we captured Leela and Molly, I think. But she went away when my little device proved too much of an obstacle. Not that she was here anyway. She was just an image projected into the room from elsewhere. A bit like a hologram."

"So where did you get this device?" asked Ivan.

"Oh, it's just a couple of apps on my phone."

"And are these apps readily available?"

"No. I wrote them. Necessity being the mother of invention, and all that." She smiled at the admiring Ivan and Zoe.

"Well! There's a skill I didn't know you had. I'm sure we can incorporate apps like that into our products. If you're willing, that is."

"Oh, or course! I'm always willing to help with new developments, as long as they're used for good."

"We'll talk about that next week. Eh?"

"Okay."

Naomi appeared in Molly and Leela's cell. She wasn't smiling.

"I found Dorranston, but they had some sort of device to keep me out of their minds. Never come across that before. I've encountered people like Torsten, who can do it by mind power, but Torsten and people like him aren't strong enough to keep me out. No, it was some sort of electronic blocking device. Damned powerful. I'll look into that another time, but for now my priority is to get you two out of here. Do you have any suggestions where to try next?"

'What about the officers here?' thought Molly. 'Surely, they've been given instructions, a list of what to do and what not to do?'

"Good thinking. Why didn't I think of that?" And with that Naomi disappeared again. She materialised on the other side of the door and walked along the corridor to the custody sergeant's desk, invisible to everyone she encountered on the way. At the main desk she made herself visible and grasped the sergeant's hand. He tried to call for help but he couldn't. She stared deep into his eyes, deep into his mind, and eventually found what she was looking for.

Back in the cell, Naomi appeared with a broad smile on her face.

"It's quite simple. The answer was staring us in the face! The device gets its power from light. Those things have solar cells on them. In the dark they don't operate. All we have to do is plunge this room into darkness and wait for the devices to run flat. You should then be free, and the final step is to remove them before someone puts the lights back on."

'Sounds simple enough,' thought Leela. 'But they are glued on and they have some sort of barbs to keep them attached.'

"That isn't going to be a problem, darling," replied Naomi. "I can remove them quickly and painlessly, once I can get my hands on them. At the moment the forcefield would hold them on, even if the glue wasn't there. Leave it to me. Now then, what's going to be the best way to put you in the dark without anyone noticing? I suppose I could put an illuminated image of the cell out into the corridor, then just throw the switch on the real cell. Yes, that's what I'll do."

'Thanks, Mum,' thought Molly. 'I knew we could count on you.'

"That's what mothers are for, sweetheart. But try to keep out of scrapes like this in future." She smiled at them and disappeared.

Moments later the cell went dark. So did the rest of the police station, for good measure. Totally dark. And it stayed dark for four or five hours. An illuminated image of the cell appeared out in the corridor, but that was a bit pointless now that everywhere else was dark.

"Damn," said Naomi to herself. "Didn't realise that switch was for the whole building. Never mind. It'll do."

# The Monastery

## Foreword

## The Monastic Offices

The following prayer times are observed by the members of the order (and the by the servants when circumstances permit) in this story. Times given would vary with the time of year:

Matins – the first office of the day, about 2am

Lauds – the first prayer after dawn, about 5am.

Prime – the first hour of the day, about 6am.

Terce – the third hour of the day, about 9am

Sext – the sixth hour of the day, about noon.

Nones – the ninth hour of the day, about 3pm

Vespers – the evening office, about 6pm

Compline – the late evening office, immediately before retiring, about 7pm

Matins, Lauds and Vespers are 'Major Hours' and would include more hymns, Psalms, prayers and Bible readings than the others.

Compline reflects preparation for death, in case they don't wake up from their sleep the next morning, which was common in those days.

## Chapter 1

It was early in the ninth century. St Columba had died some years earlier and the Christian faith he had established in Iona was slowly spreading into western Scotland and north-west parts of England, with the establishment of monasteries in his memory. Viking raids had become common along the coasts of Scotland, England and Wales, but up to now they hadn't gone very far inland. The little monastery in Cumberland was largely unaffected by these skirmishes and other forms of unrest, mainly due to its location. It was the sort of place you wouldn't pass through on the way to anywhere, even if you were lost. They got on with their business of worshipping God and helping the local people. This mainly involved growing crops of cereals and vegetables and fruit at certain times of the year which they sold in the local villages, once they had set aside some for their own needs. These places often suffered shortages, as while the rainfall was plentiful, sometimes more than plentiful, sunshine was in short supply. The monks were very successful farmers and gardeners, and their produce was always of good quality and rarely seemed to run out. They also helped the villagers with medical problems. Their herbalist, Leoric, seemed to know the answer to everything and his assistant, Rhys, who was also his chief gardener, grew whatever was needed when it was needed, and he never ran short of any herb. Every morning they had a queue of people with various complaints, some serious, some trivial, but Leoric treated them all with equal respect and managed to cure most ailments. He even managed to cure more than half of the livestock illnesses the people presented to him, but by his own admission this was largely guesswork rather than skill and knowledge. But some things don't go on for ever. One day he dragged himself along to his workshop after Prime and slumped in his chair. His assistants were concerned because they'd never before seen him in such a state. Even when he had a cold he still managed to get about and carry out his tasks, although perhaps a bit more slowly than usual. But on this day, he struggled to keep his eyes open. Rhys quickly made a cup of herbal tea, and put it to his lips, asking what else they should do. He mumbled a few words about other herbs, which Rhys instructed the others to prepare, while he tended to his patient, ensuring he had plenty to drink and was kept warm. He wondered whether this was the right thing to do, as in the past Leoric had made all the decisions, and Rhys and the others simply followed instructions. Leoric didn't complain, so they assumed they were doing right. Rhys visited Father Abbot and asked that Leoric be excused from the next time of prayer, which would be Terce. Father Abbot wasn't pleased at this idea and came down to the workshop. When he saw Leoric, he agreed with Rhys that attending prayer wouldn't be a good idea, and excused Leoric from attending prayer with the other brothers for the rest of the day, on the understanding that Leoric would pray at the appropriate times in the privacy of his workshop. This Leoric agreed to do and was faithful to this arrangement for the rest of the day, dismissing Rhys and the other helpers briefly so that his prayers would not be disturbed. After Compline they helped Leoric back to his cell and made him as comfortable as they could, despite his protestations. After a while he stopped objecting to their help. He smiled at them, thanked them for their work, said a short prayer and breathed his last.

A sadness came over the monastery. The loss of Leoric left a hole in practical terms; Rhys could do a few things, but many of what had been routine cases for Leoric were beyond the capabilities of Rhys and the others. And his parting caused sadness for many of the monks and workers. He was always kind and gentle, always provided a 'shoulder to cry on' when one was needed and was a fount of knowledge and wisdom. On more than one occasion Father Abbott had suggested these attributes would stand him well in a more senior position, but Leoric always shook his head. "If I were not here in my workshop who would heal the people?" he would say with a smile. "I would be honoured to be put into such a position, but the people need me doing what I do. That's why The Lord has put me here."

And so it proved. Rhys did his best, with help from the other workers, but quite a lot of ailments were beyond him. He went to see Father Abbott. "Begging your pardon, Father Abbott," he began, bowing and standing with his face downwards, "but our departed brother had many skills which no-one else possesses. I pray every morning that God would grant me knowledge and skill, but more recently I have simply been praying that God will grant us another Brother Leoric."

"Stand up, young Rhys," Father Abbott began. "I appreciate your concern, and I am pleased that your prayers are not for your own benefit but for the benefit of all, but people like our departed brother are few and far between. Yesterday I sent messengers away to visit three other nearby monasteries requesting that their healers visit us to give instruction to you and others so that we can make efforts to plug the hole left by our brother. Alas, the nearest is almost three days journey, so we cannot expect an answer soon, but until then God is watching over you, as you were Brother Leoric's most trusted assistant, and I am sure He will help, even though you do not realise it at the time. Carry on praying every morning and at other times. God will help us when He is ready. Be assured that I and the other monks have faith in your efforts."

"I am grateful, Father Abbott, that you and the others are supportive, and I know that God is always watching over us all, but sometimes I wish He would be more practical." There was a silence. "I'm sorry, Father Abbott, I shouldn't have said that." He looked up. "I'm sorry, Lord, for my impatience."

"Remember this sin when you are next at confession. Your sin was a momentary lapse, and was for the benefit of others, so your penance will be light. Go and do The Lord's work to the best of your ability."

Rhys bowed and returned to the workshop.

## Chapter 2

In nineteen sixty Giles was appointed to a junior professorship in archaeology at the university. He had grasped the opportunities this post provided, and as his superior struggled to get about as a result of a war wound, Giles was put in charge of field trips. One day, about a year later, he met his tutorial group in his office as usual and had a beaming smile on his face.

"Are any of you free for two or three weeks in August?" He asked them enthusiastically.

"Sorry, I'm not," Jeremy replied. "My Dad's got me a job at his firm, so I'm stuck doing that for the whole of the hols."

"I am," Edgar answered. "I haven't been able to get anything. Dad's really grumpy about it because he isn't so well off as some of the other people's folks."

"Same here," chorused Leo and Victor."

"Well, I have an opportunity for you. There'll be no money, but I will provide food and accommodation. Do you remember me telling you about that ancient religious house I discovered last summer?"

They all nodded. "The one in, er, was it Cumberland?" offered Edgar.

"That's the one. I just heard this morning they're giving me a grant to research it. Just a small grant, mind you. When I said accommodation I mean a caravan, and we'll have to cook our own food, but they will provide the raw materials."

"Sounds fab," said Victor. "I'm up for it, if you'll have me."

"Me too," added Leo. "How many are you taking?"

"Three, so it's convenient that Jeremy isn't available, because I wouldn't have been able to pick three out of you four. I'm borrowing the department's Land Rover and caravan. We need to take bottles of water because there isn't any, and the toilet will be a hole in the ground. We'll be doing our own cooking, which is a bit of a struggle for me. I can make beans on toast but that's about my limit. Are you guys still up for it?"

"Yes," they chorused, with nods and smiles all round, except for Jeremy who looked glum.

"That's going to be pants for me. Not only having to work, but missing out on a field trip too," said Jeremy.

"Hey, think of all the money you'll have! You can buy the drinks when we come back in October," said Leo with a laugh.

"Never mind, Jeremy," said Giles, trying to look consoling. "If one comes up next year during term time, I'll make sure you get first refusal."

The tutorial ran its course, then they retired to the students' union for a coffee until the bar opened.

"I don't want to go, but if I don't my dad will play hell. It'll be 'we didn't get opportunities like that when we were your age' and stuff like that," complained Edgar. "Wish I'd kept my mouth shut until he'd given us the details. Still, improves our chances of getting a good grade."

"No, it'll be fun," objected Victor. "Real field work, and it's new, so we could get our names in journals and stuff. Be famous!"

"Sounds boring," replied Edgar. "But at least it shuts the olds up about not having a job. I can tell them it's educational, I suppose, then they'll pick on my sister instead."

All the details were settled, insurance forms completed, and the three students met at the side entrance of the science block on the appointed day in July at the appointed time. They only had to wait ten minutes until Giles came round the corner in the department's Land Rover, towing the caravan. They greeted him warmly and put their bags into the back. As they got in, he gave them each a brown envelope.

"Sorry, chaps," he said with a grin. "I intended to get these to you earlier, but Beryl's been off sick, and she's the only one who can make the copier work. I tried but it was a nightmare. She just came back last week, so if I'd sent them out you wouldn't have got them in time. Anyway, let's get going and I'll tell you a bit about it on the journey and you can read it in more detail when you get fed up with the sound of my voice."

They chuckled at this. Edgar settled into a corner in the back seat and soon went to sleep. Leo sat beside him, and Victor got into the front. They set off and headed north.

"As I said the other week, it's in Cumberland," began Giles. "Any of you been to the Lake District?"

"No," answered Victor. "Our neighbour has a caravan up there and keeps offering it to us for a week or so, but my folks never take him up on it because there's hardly any shops there. Mum couldn't have a holiday without shopping." The others laughed at this, except Edgar who remained asleep.

"Well, it isn't what you would call 'mainstream' Lake District. In your envelopes there's a map showing the exact location, and the nearest 'village', which is three houses and a pub, is about fifteen miles away to the south west. That's probably why it hasn't been discovered before. I have permission from a local farmer to set up camp in his field, but he said not to expect to see anyone else. There's billycans of water in the caravan, but we need to stretch them out in case the local water isn't safe to drink. There's a little stream, so that might be okay for washing, but I'm not sure about drinking. If you find the red cross on the map, that's where the abbey is, and from there go about half a mile north and that's where we camp. Go another seven miles east and there's the farmhouse, and nothing more for about another twelve miles. It's pretty deserted, but that means we won't be disturbed by holiday makers." Giles carried on telling them about the place, but stopped when he realised he was just repeating what was in the info packs and no-one was paying much attention. He was now on unfamiliar roads, so this was a good time to stop talking so he could concentrate better. After a while he turned onto what was little more than a dirt track, and half an hour later pulled up in a field.

"Here we are, chaps!" Giles announced gleefully. They got out, having to wake Edgar up, and unhitched the caravan. Giles was obviously experienced at caravanning, and quickly had the caravan secured, and the gas bottle set up outside the kitchen window and connected up. They got their bags from the Land Rover and put them into the caravan while Giles was making a cup of tea.

"Who's sleeping where?" asked Victor.

"Those things are our seats through the day, and beds at night," said Giles. "I'm having this one." He threw his bag onto the seat by the kitchen, leaving the others to get the seats around the table by the main window.

"And where's the toilet?" asked Edgar.

Giles opened a cupboard by the door and produced a garden trowel in a plastic bag. "Hole in the ground," he announced. "And there's toilet paper to wipe it before putting it back in the bag. And don't dig your hole too close to the windows. Best do it on the other side of the Land Rover. That way you'll have a bit of privacy." They finished unloading their bags and sat down around the table. "Anyone hungry?" asked Giles. They nodded. "Okay. You're going to experience my speciality. Beans on toast." They glanced at one another but found the beans on toast acceptable when washed down with a small bottle of beer. "I suggest we get some sleep, because tomorrow you'll see some amazing things." They turned in, unable to sleep because of the absolute silence.

## Chapter 3

Father Abbott had returned to his cell and was preparing a Bible study for the junior monks, when there was a knock at the door.

"Come!" he called, and a servant entered, followed by an unfamiliar figure.

"Sorry to disturb you, Father," the servant said, his face turned to the floor.

"Stand up, Alfred," said Father Abbott. "Who is this?"

"This is Brother Alwern, Father. He has just arrived, so I thought it would be best to bring him to meet you straight away."

"You did right, my son. Leave us and return to your duties." The young man bowed and left, closing the door behind him. "Greetings, Brother Alwern. May the Lord's blessing be upon you. What brings you to our humble monastery?"

The monk bowed. "May His blessings be on you also, and on this place. I have been sent here. I understand you are in need of a healer. The Lord has blessed me with healing skills. I also have teaching skills, and can instruct one of your brothers, or perhaps two, so that they can replace me when I leave."

Father Abbott's face broke into a smile. "You are most welcome. Our healing brother, Brother Leoric, passed away and we have been without a healer since then. Rhys, his main servant, has led a small team, and they have had successes with minor ailments, but are unable to heal those with serious illnesses. It is almost time for our next meal. Come to the refectory, then after Sext I will instruct someone to find you a cell and show you Brother Leoric's workshop. I must stop calling it that, but that is how everyone knows it. It will become 'Brother Alwern's workshop' from this day forward."

Alwern smiled and followed Father Abbott to the refectory. When they entered the company rose to their feet. Father Abbott had an extra stool brought to the table and instructed everyone to sit. He remained standing and smiled warmly. "Brothers," he began, "and others of this place, the Lord has smiled upon us. It was a sad day when we saw the demise of Brother Leoric, in many ways, but today, Brother Alwern," he gestured to the new monk, "has joined us, sent by the Lord whom we worship to be our new healing brother. He will instruct one or two people, perhaps a brother and a lay man, in healing, and they shall replace him when he moves on. Bring in the repast." He sat and the servants brought in the meagre meal and served it to the company. After a prayer they began to eat. "Rhys, come here please." Rhys approached the table. "This is Rhys. He was Brother Leoric's trusted servant and has some healing skills. I hope you will find him a good assistant. After Sext he will show you where everything is in the workshop and medicinal garden. I will identify a suitable brother to be your understudy, and Brother Jerome will see to it that your cell is satisfactory and you are cared for regarding your spiritual needs. Go and eat, Rhys, and seek out our new brother after Sext."

Rhys bowed and returned to his seat. The servants were keen to know what was happening, and Rhys began to tell them, but Father Abbott stopped the chatter and insisted on silence for the rest of the meal. While they were clearing the dishes away Rhys told them what he could in the short time available, then they went to the chapel for Sext, after which

Rhys joined Brother Alwern and led him away. They were joined by three others who had worked in Leoric's garden and workshop and made their way to the south side of the monastery. On the way Alwern said few words to the others, but to Rhys' amazement he seemed to know the way, taking every corner before being told, and reaching the workshop in a short time without deviating from the route. Rhys invited his companions to introduce themselves and to explain which aspects of the herbs they were responsible for. Alwern smiled all the while and thanked them for their husbandry of the herbs. Just as they finished and Rhys was wondering what to say next Brother Jerome, second only to Father Abbott, appeared through the arched entrance to the garden and offered to take Alwern to see his new cell. The servants stood just looking at one another as the two monks departed.

"Is it me or is he a bit strange?" said Egbert quietly once they were away from the garden. "I mean, he seems nice, very nice, but did you notice how we didn't need to show him the way?"

"Yes, I noticed that, but don't call him strange. He is a Brother," replied Rhys.

"No disrespect intended, Rhys, but he didn't seem, well, normal somehow."

"I agree with Egbert," said Athel. "He does seem nice, but there's something odd about him."

"Well, it isn't our job to question our superiors. It's our job to do our work, so let's get on with it. If Brother Jerome were to come back and find us chatting, he'd have something to say to Father Abbott, and it wouldn't be anything good. We all know what he's like."

"Yes. Let's get on with it. We want the garden to look good for the new Brother."

Chapter 4

The next morning, they got up and converted their beds back into seats while Giles made breakfast. He could cook eggs and bacon without it going wrong, and they all enjoyed it. Over breakfast he outlined his plans for the day.

"This morning I want to go to the monastery and become accustomed to what is where and do some rough sketches of floor plans. After lunch, which will be back here, we'll go back and do some detailed drawings and floor plans with measurements and copy down what appear to be inscriptions on the floors. Some are runic, some Greek and some are Latin, which is a bit puzzling, but once we've got it translated, we might have a clue about what went on before it closed down. There are some paraffin lanterns in the Land Rover, which we need to fill up from the jerry can under the kitchen and make sure they're working before we set off."

"Lanterns?" queried Victor. "But it's daylight. Why would we need lanterns? I can understand taking one, but four?"

"It's dark in lots of places. You'll see," Giles replied with a grin. They filled the lanterns and tested them and set off across the field. "Nearly there," said Giles as they walked up a gentle incline. When they breached the top of the rise they saw what looked like a huge rock in front of them. Giles smiled broadly and gesticulated at it. "Here we are. We've arrived. This is it!" He grinned broadly while the others looked confused.

"Er, where is it?" asked Leo. "Is that it?" He pointed at the rock.

"Yes and no," replied Giles. "It's in there."

"What, inside the rock?" asked Victor.

"Exactly. That's why we need the lanterns. The rock hides the entrance to the monastery, which is partly inside and partly underneath. Come on."

They scrambled down the fell-side and at the bottom they saw what looked like the entrance to a cave. They lit the lanterns and went inside. Giles pressed on boldly, lantern held aloft, while the others proceeded more cautiously. They were in a cavernous space, with a ceiling at least fifty feet above floor level. As they raised their lanterns they could see a doorway at the opposite side, flanked by stone statues. Giles walked briskly towards it, and the others followed. He stopped at the statues.

"I would like whoever is best at drawing to draw these chaps, but not now. This afternoon. Come on." He turned away and went through the doorway. They followed, no-one wanting to be the last one in the cavern. There weren't any obvious hazards, but the three didn't feel comfortable. Further in there was a large room with four arched doorways leading into blackness. "This way!" called Giles, heading into one of them. They followed and found a bigger room with a strange design carved into the floor near the window. Around it were small primitive stone tables, each with a rack next to it. "I'm assuming this is the scriptorium, where the monks would copy out Bibles and other documents. These racks here, they could hold the book being copied while the monk used the little table to hold his vellum and pens etc. Come on – more to see." He turned and went off through a doorway at the far end. "This I believe is the library," he said, when they had caught up. There are several shelves, with marks where metal has ground the edge away, probably from where the books were secured in place by chains. Books were very valuable and they wouldn't leave them laid about." He turned and went back to the large room. From there they explored a refectory with what might be an adjoining kitchen, two dormitories, twelve cells, three workshops and a chapel with more statues. Giles specified what they were to do in each room when they returned after lunch.

Back at the caravan, Leo was preparing vegetable soup (from cans) for lunch when they heard the sound of a motorcycle. Giles went out to investigate. It was a messenger, who removed his helmet and took an envelope from the inside pocket of his leather jacket.

"Are you Professor Worthington?" he asked. Giles nodded. "Then this is for you, sir. Do you want me to take a reply?"

Giles opened the envelope, read it, and nodded again. "Dear me! Yes, just a minute." He went back inside and scribbled a note which he gave to the messenger and thanked him. The man drove off.

Back in the caravan he sat down with his head in his hands. "What's up, Giles?" asked Victor.

"Sorry, chaps," he replied. "I have to go home urgently. My wife's taken ill and I need to sort out some childcare for the baby, and help for my mother-in-law. Do you want to stay here? I've told you what needs doing, and I can be back on Friday to take you home on Saturday. Providing I can sort out help, that is."

"I hope it's nothing serious, but yes, I'm willing to stay, if the others are," said Victor. The other two nodded.

"Good. No, it's nothing serious, but she needs to go into hospital for an urgent operation. Quite minor, but urgent. We don't have any family close by, apart from her mother, who isn't safe to be left alone, so I'll have to organise paid help for a few days. It isn't a problem – we've done it before, but I need to be home to sort it all out. The people I want to contact don't have telephones. And I'm not sure where the nearest one is here either."

"Right," said Leo. "Have some of this soup. It'll set you up for the journey. It's ready now."

Giles tucked into a bowl of soup and a slice of bread while the others removed from the Land Rover what they might need and put together some sandwiches and a flask of tea for the journey. Giles had a look in the back of the vehicle and transferred a few other things they'd overlooked that he thought they might need and set off.

"Well, that's a bit of an unexpected turn up," said Victor while they devoured the soup. "I hope Mrs W is going to be okay. I've only met her once, but she seemed really nice."

"Yes. But we've a job on our hands without Giles to keep us right," replied Leo. "I know he told us what he wants us to do, but I've never been on one of these without someone to keep me right."

"Oh, we'll be okay," said Edgar. "If there's something we're not sure about, we just leave that bit and move on to the next thing."

"You mean use it as an excuse to skive?" said Leo. "I don't know why you took this course. You never seem to show any enthusiasm or interest."

"No, I didn't want to do it, but two of my A-levels turned out worse than expected, and the other one much better than expected, and my original preference wouldn't accept me, so it was do this or don't go to uni and end up working for one of the old man's pals in some drudge job or other."

"Tough luck. But let's finish this soup and get back to the monastery. If we get everything done before Giles gets back it will help our grades," said Victor. They finished their soup and set off back up the hill armed with lanterns, tape measure, paper and pencils.

## Chapter 5

Brother Alwern thanked Brother Jerome for his help and unpacked his bag. It contained a change of clothing and a small book.

"What's this?" asked Brother Jerome. "We aren't permitted books for personal use. I'll take it and put it in the library." He reached out to grasp it, but Brother Alwern stopped him.

"No, Brother, this is not for personal use. This is for the use of my team. It needs to reside in the workshop. It contains many things few would understand, and in the wrong hands it could be dangerous."

"All the more reason to keep it safe. Suppose someone in the workshop tried to use it."

"Rhys seems quite sensible, but I doubt he can read. Whereas those who frequent the library, the brothers, can all read to a greater or lesser extent. No, it must remain in the workshop."

"As you wish, but I will make Father Abbott aware of your contravention of our rules on your first day. He will not be pleased."

"Thank-you, Brother. I am pleased to note that you do everything you can to ensure people observe the rules of the monastery. I will make Father Abbott aware of your strict obedience. Now I must return to the workshop. I have people to heal and much to learn about which herbs we have, and which we lack." He put the little book into the pocket of his habit and left. He walked quickly and Brother Jerome soon lost sight of him.

The next day after Terce Brother Alwern went to the scriptorium and asked Brother Ambrose, the senior Brother there, for a mason to carry out a task. After some discussion Brother Ambrose addressed the monks there to allay their concerns, and a junior brother was allocated to the task. Brother Alwern set him to work on the floor between the middle of the room and the window. He took a piece of chalk from his pocket and wrote on the floor three lines of text and instructed the Brother to chisel the letters out.

"With respect, Brother, I do not understand the second line, which looks like Greek, and the third line is, well, it's just lines, which don't appear to form letters."

"Do not worry, Brother. They are letters beyond your experience. There are times when we must do the Lord's work without needing to understand it.

"This is the Lord's work?"

"It is."

"Then I shall begin immediately."

"Thank-you. If anyone questions what you are doing, tell them Brother Arwen is instructing you and it is the Lord's work. We have the support of Brother Ambrose for this important task."

As they were leaving the refectory after the mid-day meal Brother Jerome took Father Abbott aside.

"Father Abbott, I am sure you know what you are doing, but I understand Brother Barnabas is to be Brother Alwern's pupil. Do you think this is wise? I remember having some difficulty with Brother Barnabas on more than one occasion, and indeed, I was not in favour of him becoming a brother when he first made that important step, a step which I felt at the time was beyond him."

"Brother Jerome, thank-you for reminding me. I had not forgotten. I try to remember everything, and I recall at the time he was without parents and we, the monastery that is, had a duty to care for him in his childhood, and I saw a flicker of goodness in him as he approached adulthood. I think his tutelage under the new Brother will be the making of him. His behaviour is altogether better when he has a specific objective to his work."

"I hope you know what you are doing, Father Abbott."

"Brother Jerome, this decision about Brother Barnabas was not mine."

"So Brother Alwern is doing things without your approval!"

"Not so, Brother. The decision was not mine alone. I prayed long and hard about Brother Barnabas, on this occasion and others, and what I have done is to carry out instructions from Almighty God, so if you think what I've done is wrong, you'd better have a word with God. I trust you will remember this conversation next time you make confession."

Brother Jerome fell to his knees. "Forgive me, Father." He looked up to the ceiling. "Forgive me, Lord. You alone are perfect. I am your imperfect servant trying to do what is right." He made the sign of the cross and stood up. Father Abbott gave him a gentle hug and dismissed him.

Brother Arwen returned to his workshop where Rhys and the others were tending the gardens. He addressed Rhys.

"Come, Rhys. Bring a basket and a trowel. We must forage for what we do not have. I am certain most of them will be nearby." He turned and left. Rhys grabbed the basket and trowel and hastened after him.

"Where are we going, Brother?" he asked.

"To the meadow beyond the woods. I saw it on my way here and made a note that it would be a good place for herbs."

They crossed the small wood and as they emerged on the other side Brother Arwen stopped suddenly. He closed his eyes for a moment, turned to his left, and set off at speed. "Come! This way!" he called as Rhys ran to try to keep up. Once again, he stopped suddenly. He pointed to his left at a small yellow flower. "Dig this up carefully, making sure there is plenty of root, and put it in the basket." Rhys did as instructed then they moved on. Brother Arwen pointed to another and gave the same instruction, which Rhys obeyed. At the next plant Brother Arwen said, "Take three petals and five leaves from this plant. We must not take the plant; it would kill the others." Rhys complied.

"Why would it kill the others?" he asked.

"It would take all the nutrients and those around it would starve to death."

"So why do they all thrive here?"

"Observe its place. There are no other plants around it for the distance of a man's foot. They cannot grow near it."

"Oh, I see."

"It is good that you ask such questions. It shows me you want to learn. That is good. One day you might be a good healer."

"But I am not a brother, and I am not as clever as you."

"Would you like to be a brother?"

Rhys thought for a while. "I'm not sure. It would mean learning letters and numbers and things from books. I enjoy being your servant and assistant, but I'm not sure about anything complicated."

"Do not worry, Rhys. You are young. There is time." They pressed on gathering sometimes whole plants, sometimes just flowers and leaves and berries and twigs. They returned to the monastery just in time for Nones. Rhys thanked Brother Arwen for what he had learned that day.

## Chapter 6

They tramped up the incline, Leo and Victor chatting happily, Edgar following on in silence. At the top they paused for breath before going down to the entrance, where they lit the lanterns and went inside.

"Let's do the floor plans first, then we can split up and do individual tasks," suggested Victor. The others agreed, so Leo made a rough sketch, then Edgar and Victor took measurements, which Victor wrote down. Then they went to the next room and repeated the exercise, moving through the building slowly. The last room to measure was one of what Giles thought might be a workshop, and they sat down for a rest while Leo made notes. They were just getting up when they saw a figure in the doorway. Even with the lanterns, the room was dark, but they knew it wasn't Giles. Despite the dim light they could tell he was dressed in a monk's habit.

"Er, hello. Who are you?" asked Victor.

"You are obviously puzzled. I am your guide," the man answered, bowing slightly.

"What, you mean like in a museum?"

"I don't know. I can tell you what things are and which room you are in. I might be able to answer some of your questions."

"Fab. Giles didn't mention you."

"Giles?"

"The prof. He was here months ago, and he was here this morning, but he had to go home. He found this place."

"Found? But it has never been lost." The three laughed at that, but the man didn't understand what was funny. "No matter. What do you want to know?"

They looked at one another, wondering what to ask. "Well, what room are we in now?" Victor asked hesitantly.

"This was the healing brother's workshop. This is where he prepared medicines from herbs and minerals."

"Wow! That's great," said Victor, much to the man's surprise. "So how many people would be working in this room?"

"There would be the healing brother, and he would have two servants, sometimes three, and they would work in here and in the garden in the courtyard, tending the herbs. Sick people would be brought here for healing. But the brother would leave the workshop to go to the chapel for the office services. The servants would go too, when they didn't have a sick person to care for, but at least once a day. Come. Follow." And he turned away and walked through an archway into another room, then he stopped suddenly and inclined his head, as though listening intently. He turned back to them. "I must away," he said urgently. "I will return." And with that he walked off at incredible speed through the next archway. The three tried to follow him, but even at a trot they couldn't keep up, and he turned off into another room. They tried to follow, but when they got there, he was nowhere to be seen.

"That's odd," said Leo, who was ahead of the others. "Very odd. He definitely came in here, and this is the only doorway, and now he's vanished."

"Sounds like a stupid question," began Victor, "But he was here, wasn't he? I mean, is he real? Or did we just imagine him?"

"None of us touched him, but we all saw him," replied Edgar. "I definitely saw him. No jesting."

"He said he would be back, so I suggest we get on with our tasks for now, and we can ask next time we see him," said Victor. They retraced their steps and Leo went back to the entrance to draw the statues while Edgar and Victor went to the scriptorium to copy out the letters scratched into the floor. The Latin inscription was easy as the letters were very similar to what they were used to. The Greek inscription was a little more difficult, as none of them was familiar with the language and some letters were difficult to decipher. The third line took quite a while, as they didn't recognise it at all, and Leo rejoined them long before they were finished.

Two days later they saw the monk again. They had been diligently following Giles' instructions and had managed to achieve most of his tasks without any problems. Victor was sketching the walls of the library, as the floor plan didn't tell the entire story. He drew each wall, showing the number of shelves, their spacing, and recording the locations of the indentations from the chains. Leo had drawn, to the best of his abilities, the statues in the chapel, and Edgar had recorded the locations of a small number of artefacts such as knives and chisels. They had just arrived back at the dig after lunch when the monk greeted them at the doorway.

"Come," he said. "I will show you something you have not seen." He led them at speed into the chapel. When they caught up with him, he was on his knees at the altar, praying, and he stood up as they approached. He beckoned them to follow as he squeezed between the altar and the wall. He indicated marks on the floor, which on closer inspection revealed a stone rectangle. "Under there you will find many interesting things." So saying, he disappeared. The three men looked at each other for a moment, then Victor bent down to try to move it. He could move it a fraction of an inch by applying all his strength to it while the others looked on.

"Sorry, mate," said Edgar with a grin. "There isn't room enough for us to join you. My suggestion is to come back tomorrow with some tools. I'm sure I saw a crowbar and a couple of chisels in the caravan."

"Good idea, Ed," said Leo. "Let's see if this altar moves. That would give us a bit more space."

They tried dragging it away from the wall, levering themselves against the wall, and turning it from the side, but the altar remained immobile. They sat on the floor to get their breaths back, then Victor, who wasn't usually defeated by something as small as a big stone altar, agreed that Edgar's idea was more likely to succeed than anything else.

"Let's call it a day," he said. "Tomorrow's Friday, so with any luck Giles will be back, and he might have some ideas about what to do.

## Chapter 7

As they left the chapel after Vespers Father Abbott approached Brother Arwen. "Walk with me a while," he said, and they walked slowly towards their cells and let the others get ahead. When everyone else was out of earshot Father Abbott broached the subject of the inscription on the floor of the scriptorium. "I myself have not yet visited the scriptorium, as I have many pressing duties, but some of the Brothers are perplexed by your inscription. Indeed, anger has been expressed in some quarters."

"Alas, my actions are not always welcome," Brother Arwen commented without raising his head.

"Tell me, Brother, what the Latin inscription says. Three Brothers have each given me a different translation. I was under the impression that all Brothers were fluent in Latin; perhaps this is not so."

It says, 'Dei semper eterna sunt' - the things of God are always everlasting."

Father Abbot pondered on this for a moment. "I thought that would be self-explanatory and wouldn't need to be written anywhere."

"Ah, Father Abbott, yes, it is self-explanatory to you and me, and I would expect to the other Brothers too, but this is not for us. It is for those yet to come. Future peoples might need to be reminded, or even to have this pointed out to them."

"You mean that when we have passed over there will be peoples who are not so enlightened?"

"Exactly so, Father Abbott. Exactly so."

"And what makes you think this will be the case?"

"I have prayed long and hard about this, and many other things, and the Lord God Almighty has instructed me to do this thing, and others, for the benefit of those who will come here when we are long gone."

"Good. If God has instructed you I will question it no further. And I will tell others not to question it."

"Thank-you, Father Abbott. Everything I do is either on God's instruction or to fulfil His requirements. Understanding the future is both a blessing and a curse."

"A curse?

"Sometimes I must do things I find, er, distasteful or unpleasant, but when they are God's commands, I must do them."

"I see. And what of the Greek?"

"It is the same."

"But Brother Jerome can read Greek better than I can!"

"You did mention earlier, Father Abbott, that anger has been expressed. I am aware that Brother Jerome is fluent in Greek. But there are times when it is easier to feign ignorance than to tax the mind."

"I will speak to him about this."

"No, Father Abbott. I have already forgiven him, and I have asked God to forgive him. There is no need to pursue this matter further."

"As you wish." They walked on in silence for a moment, then Father Abbott spoke again. "And the third line of script?"

"It is runic. The language of the Viking people."

Father Abbott stopped suddenly. "The Viking people? But they are our enemies, and they are pagans, worshipping strange gods and rejecting Christ! I have heard that they destroy our homes, take our crops and kill our people."

"At present, yes. But in the future, they will be our friends and will live among us and will worship Christ just as we do. I have seen it"

"In the future?"

"Indeed."

"You are truly enlightened, Brother Arwen. Thank-you for enlightening me. We are at my cell now, and I must pray and study before supper. You have given me much to pray about. Until supper." They bowed slightly and Brother Arwen continued to his own cell.

As they gathered for Compline Brother Jerome took Father Abbott aside. "Have you seen what Brother Ambrose has permitted him to put on the floor of the scriptorium?"

"I take it you are talking about Brother Arwen?"

"I am indeed!"

"Brother Arwen has my support in this matter and in several others. He is greatly enlightened, and everything he does is on God's command or for God's purpose. I suggest you prepare your mind for Compline, Brother Jerome."

"Yes, but," Father Abbott held up his hand.

"I wish to prepare myself for Compline, even if you do not, Brother. Think about this at your next confession and think about what is written on the scriptorium floor."

"Yes, Father." Jerome went away, disgruntled. As they left Compline Brother Jerome tried to speak to Brother Ambrose. "Don't you see, Brother? He is trying to poison Father Abbott's mind!"

"Brother Jerome, it is our custom to remain silent for the rest of the day after Compline. I wish to comply with this custom. Please leave me in peace."

Brother Jerome left him and walked quickly up the line, catching up with Brother Arwen. "Brother Arwen, I see what you are trying to do, and I will not let it happen," he hissed. The other brothers shushed him, and Arwen ignored him completely. When they reached Arwen's cell he stopped, turned to face Jerome, made the sign of the cross, and disappeared. Jerome suddenly found himself alone in the corridor, Arwen's cell being at the end.

The next morning Brother Jerome was up before Matins and went down to Arwen's workshop, hoping to find something amiss to report to Father Abbott, but everything was in order. He set off back towards the chapel and paused at the corner of the corridor. He stood there in silence, wondering if Arwen had broken any rules, no matter how obscure, when he heard voices talking and laughing. "That must be some of the servants making a noise. I'll soon sort them out!" he muttered to himself angrily. He made off back along the corridor to where he thought the voices were coming from. He passed the corridor leading to the servants' quarters and following the sound continued toward the workshops. "What on earth are they doing there at this time of the morning?" he muttered under his breath. As he approached the herb garden, he saw some young men in the corridor along the opposite wall. Except there wasn't usually a corridor there. Through the arches he was sure he could see three young men, walking along, and talking as they went. But it was still dark, and he couldn't see who they were. They didn't look like any of the servants, and that corridor wasn't supposed to be there anyway, nor were the arches through which he could see them. He felt sure the corridor and archway weren't there three days ago which was the last time he had been in this part of the monastery. He didn't come here often, as he tried to avoid Brother Arwen. Arwen always seemed to be up to something, but even he couldn't create a new corridor in one day. What should he do? Should he investigate, or return to his cell? It would soon be time for Matins and he didn't want to be late – that would be playing into Arwen's hands. He settled on a plan. That night after Compline when there was no-one about he would prepare a torch and leave it in the herb garden, with a flint and some kindling so he could light it, should the men return. Yes, that would be a good idea, and if it was Arwen he would catch him red-handed, and if it wasn't, well, he would catch someone else red-handed. He returned to the chapel and got there just in time for Matins.

## Chapter 8

The three had the remains of the bacon and eggs, gathered up the crowbar, chisels and a decent hammer, and made their way to the monastery. They returned to the chapel and tried to prise the rectangular stone using the crowbar at one side and the biggest chisel at the other. It moved a fraction of an inch, but they weren't quick enough and it fell back into its place. After a brief discussion they tried levering all from the same end. The stone block lifted about a foot at one end, and Leo grabbed a piece of masonry to hold it open while they took a breather. More heaving and levering raised it to the point where it stood up on one end, and they could see a few roughly hewn stone steps leading down into a place which wasn't totally dark, but too dark to see. After positioning more rocks to make sure the stone stayed up, they returned to the caravan and made some lunch, planning to return with freshly filled lanterns, as two had already run out of paraffin, and the other wasn't looking too promising. They were about to set off back (with replenished lanterns) when they heard the sound of an engine. It was Giles in the Land Rover. He parked up and came into the caravan, greeted them warmly, and sat down to eat a sandwich he had in his bag. His wife was now over the worst, and a helpful neighbour was looking after the baby and mother-in-law. They told him about the progress they had made with his task list, and he was pleased until they mentioned the monk.

"Sorry, chaps," he said. "I haven't a clue what you're talking about. There shouldn't be anyone here apart from us. When I discovered it much of it was under soil, and it was totally isolated, silent like the grave. I'm concerned that someone is trying to muscle in on my discovery."

The others glanced at each other. "Well, he didn't give us that impression," said Victor. "He said he was here to be our guide, so we thought you had organised him. He really seemed to know what's what. He could tell us what each room was used for and guided us in and out as though he'd been there for years."

"Be that as it may, I'm not happy about this. I've finished lunch, such as it was, so if you're ready, let's get down there and see what he's up to." He picked up the fourth lantern, noticed it was almost out of fuel, and topped it up while the others visited 'the facilities' behind the Land Rover. He strode off at speed with Leo and Victor trying to talk to him and Edgar lagging behind. At the entrance they stopped to light the lanterns, then cautiously stepped into the first room. They progressed through all the rooms, about twenty in total, glancing into the cells along the corridor, about twelve of them, then followed the corridor to the chapel. Victor was keen to show Giles the steps behind the altar, and Giles was delighted, as he hadn't known about this. He led the way down, followed by Victor and Leo. Edgar stood at the top, in case anything went wrong, and took the opportunity to sit and have a cigarette.

Down in the undercroft, as Giles called it, there were several archways which had been blocked off by uneven stones, until they got to the far end, where there was an unblocked archway. They went through and it suddenly opened up into a quadrangle, lit by the sun. They looked around in disbelief for a moment and took a few steps along the corridor, then went back through the arch. They stared at one another for a few minutes. "Did you see what I saw?"

asked Giles. Leo and Victor both nodded. "Shall we try it again?" They nodded again, and gingerly stepped through the archway into the sunshine. Shielding their eyes until they adjusted, they saw people on the opposite side of the quad. About seven or eight were dressed as monks, and Victor and Leo quickly spotted their guide. They pointed to him, and their sudden movements attracted the attention of the monks, who were alarmed by the presence of the newcomers. Their guide came across to talk to them, followed by an angry-looking monk, who spoke in a strange language while he gesticulated wildly. The guide monk tried to calm him down, and he stopped advancing, but remained angry and shouting.

"What's he saying?" Victor whispered to Giles. "I can't understand a word of it."

"I can't understand much," Giles answered in a whisper. "It sounds to me like Old English, but I'm not fluent; just the odd word. I think he's blaming the other monk for us being here and telling him to do something. I can't make out the rest of it – too complicated for me." They walked slowly backwards to the arch, and as they stepped through it the people disappeared, as did the sunshine.

"Wow!" said Leo. "What's going on, Giles? We were expecting historic finds, but nothing like this!"

"Yes," said Giles slowly, stroking his chin. "I'm not sure whether to be excited or worried by what just happened. Stay here. I want to try something. Keep your eyes peeled and make a mental note of everything you see." He went to the archway, then very slowly stepped through it. The earlier scene immediately came back to life, with the guide monk and the angry monk looking at him. At his appearance the angry monk started gesticulating and shouting again. Giles stepped back through the archway, and it all disappeared. He turned to face Leo and Victor, who were standing open-mouthed. "What's wrong?" Giles asked. "What did you see?"

"Nothing," answered Leo. "Absolutely nothing. We were just about to panic when you came back."

"What do you mean? As soon as I went through the arch the scene came back, with the people and the monks."

Leo and Victor shook their heads. "No, it didn't," said Victor. "As soon as you went through the arch you disappeared, and we were left staring at a hole in the wall just full of blackness."

Giles scratched his head for a moment. "This is very strange. I'm tempted to ask one of you to go through, but I'm not sure the insurance would cover it."

"Not sure the insurance would cover it? What do you mean by that?" asked Leo.

"He means if you went through and didn't come back, he'd have a lot of paperwork to do because the university would be liable and the insurance wouldn't compensate your olds," answered Victor.

"Nice," said Leo. They turned to Giles, who shrugged his shoulders.

"That sums it up rather well, Vic. Have you considered a career in law?" Giles commented.

Victor ignored that last remark. "But despite that, I'm willing to give it a go. But not as far as we went the first time – only a little way in," he said cheerfully. He stepped forward to the arch and stopped. He clenched his fists. "Here goes!" He stepped forward into the archway and disappeared. Giles and Leo looked at each other, then ran to the archway. They could see nothing. Blackness.

Victor emerged onto the edge of the quadrangle, where everything became as it had been earlier. It didn't take the angry monk long to spot him and run forward. Victor quickly turned and ran back through the arch into the safety of the undercroft, but this time he was followed by the angry monk who came through then stopped suddenly, his expression one of fear mixed with disbelief. After staring at the three men from another century he turned and fled back to his own time. They chuckled briefly, then Giles took on a stern expression.

"Well, chaps, this is rather an unusual situation. Where do we go from here?"

## Chapter 9

On the day when Brother Jerome had hatched his plan, on his way back from Matins he prepared a small torch, some kindling and a flint and striker, as planned, and hid them in a corner of the herb garden behind some tools. He returned to the refectory where breakfast was being prepared. Arwen was carrying on with his usual procedures, instructing Rhys and his little team with the day's activities. Jerome sat down to breakfast, keeping an eye on Brother Arwen all the time. After Lauds he attended to a few minor matters then made his way to Arwen's workshop, making sure no-one saw him until he arrived in the quadrangle. He slowly walked across to the herb garden, and Arwen spotted him. He approached with a warm smile.

"Good morning, Brother. It isn't often we see you down here. Are you in need of our ministrations?"

"No, thank-you, Brother. I am quite well," he replied, trying to be civil but not friendly. "I was just …" But he didn't complete his sentence. The corridor and archway had appeared on the opposite wall, and a strange man walked through it into the quadrangle. Jerome pointed at him. "Look! Who's that? What's he doing here? Is this your doing, Brother Arwen? Are we in danger? I'll speak to Father Abbott about this!" The man disappeared.

"Why, no. It isn't any of my doing. I will accompany you to Father Abbott to help recount the event. Come, let us go to him now."

This was not what Jerome wanted. He would be deprived of his opportunity to put the blame onto Arwen. But he had no alternative, so they ran along to Father Abbott's cell, where they found him on his knees, praying. He finished his prayer while they waited, then got to his feet and greeted them. The cell was rather small for three men, so he suggested they sit in the refectory, which was the nearest big room. Brother Jerome related what had happened, and Brother Arwen nodded.

"Father Abbott, I came along to vouch for Brother Jerome, to assure you that he isn't making anything up, and isn't suffering any strangeness of the mind," said Arwen gravely. Brother Jerome clenched his fists, growled and stamped off.

Father Abbott sighed. "Thank-you for coming to vouch for our Brother, but I fear you know more than you are telling. What do you have to say?"

"Cast your mind back to shortly after I arrived, Father. I said then that I knew of things from the future. These are such things. I can show you if you wish, but I think it might disturb your mind, yes, even your great intellect, so I would advise against it. I will take steps to prevent our visitors returning. This world is theirs, but this time is not. They are explorers who have somehow broken through their boundaries and transgressed ours." With that he turned and left the refectory. Father Abbott tried to follow but he was nowhere to be seen. The old man returned to his cell and sat on the edge of his bed in thought for a while. After praying on his knees for over an hour he got up and went in search of Brother Jerome.

Brother Jerome had returned to the quadrangle next to Arwen's herb garden and stood with hands on hips, surveying all around, looking for something amiss and becoming more and more angry as he continued to find everything in order. He crossed the grass to the wall where the extra corridor had appeared and felt along the stones of the wall.

"What are you doing, Brother?" came a voice from behind him. He jumped. It was Brother Arwen.

"Oh, er, I was just checking the soundness of this wall, in case it contained a hidden defect," he replied sheepishly.

"You will not find what you seek, Brother," said Arwen. "I have already sought a breach and found none." Jerome turned to face him, but he had disappeared. Jerome began to make his way back, as it would soon be time for Prime, but he heard a noise behind him. Out of the corner of his eye he spied one the strange men. He turned and gave chase. The man disappeared through the hole in the wall, which closed. Jerome was running too quickly to stop himself and he ran into it. It gave way under his pressure, and he fell through. Before him were the three men he had seen earlier. He was speechless with fear and ran back to his own time. He fled across the quadrangle and headed for the chapel. He was almost there when he ran into Father Abbott, quite literally, almost knocking the elderly monk off his feet. He grabbed him to make sure he didn't fall, then threw himself to his knees at Father Abbott's feet. He clung to the Father's habit and wept copiously. Father Abbott tried to drag Jerome to his feet and pushed him onto a side room.

"What is this about, Brother? Why so distressed?"

Brother Jerome continued to weep. "Forgive me, Father, for I have sinned. I have sinned so greatly that I do not deserve to remain in this order."

Father Abbott picked him up and pushed him onto a seat and sat beside him. "Tell me, Brother, how you have sinned, and how you know it is a great sin."

"Father, I have seen unspeakable things. Things which should not be. Things which can only be the works of the devil. My sins must be great and many for such visions to be visited upon me. You must expel me from this holy order, lest I taint the other brothers."

Father Abbott managed to calm him down and persuaded him to recount the latest events. "No, Brother Jerome," he said when he had heard the tale. "Alas, these were not visions. These are things which really took place. Brother Arwen has told me of such and is trying to close the portal so that they trouble us no longer. Be assured you are not wicked. These are not sins, just events that you were unfortunate to experience." He stood up and made the sign of the cross in front of Jerome's face. "*Absolvo te*," he said solemnly, and kissed the top of his head.

"Thank-you, Father, I feel much better. If these were real events, as you say they were, they are of such frightening nature that the younger brothers and the servants would be scared out of their wits."

"Quite, and those of age and experience too. That is why Brother Arwen is trying to close the portal. He says they will do no harm to us, but will cause great alarm, as you have pointed out. I suggest you go to the chapel and pray until the next appointed time for prayer." Brother Jerome rose to his feet, bowed solemnly, and went to the chapel. Father Abbott shook his head. "Alas, Brother Jerome warned me that there was more to our new Brother than met the eye, and I didn't listen to him, because he oft sees the bad where there isn't any. Perhaps he is sometime wiser than I credit." He slowly walked off and joined Brother Jerome in the chapel.

## Chapter 10

They were wondering what to do next when the guide monk appeared through the archway. Giles stepped forward.

"I don't want to be difficult, but I think we deserve some answers," he said.

"Please ask," said the guide monk. "I will try to answer."

"Well, er, for a start, how come we can understand you but not your colleague? And what is on the other side of that archway?"

"The archway takes you back about a thousand years. Brother Jerome has not travelled as I have and doesn't speak modern English. Any more?"

"How come we can all travel through it? Is it some sort of magic portal?"

"Yes, it is a portal, but magic – no."

"Could we get stuck on the other side? How come you haven't got stuck?"

"Yes, if you stayed on the other side for too long you might not be able to return. I am the creator and keeper of the portal. I will never get stuck. I have tried to help with information about the monastery. Is there anything else you wish to know?"

"Not at the moment, thanks. You have been very helpful, but we still don't understand how it all works."

"Do you wish to spend more time on the other side? If you do, you must return when I say, or you will become stuck there forever."

"That would be wonderful. When can we start?"

"We can start now, but when I say it is time to go, it is time to go."

"Splendid! Let's get on with it."

The guide monk stepped into the archway and beckoned them to follow. He went further in, and as they followed the earlier scene appeared, with monks and others. He explained to the other monks that he had *bona fide* visitors and was showing them around the monastery. Most of the monks were alarmed, but he told them not to worry. Of course, Giles and the students couldn't understand what he said, as he spoke in Old English, but Giles could pick out the odd word here and there. After the tour he turned to them and said, "Come. We must away, or you will remain here for ever." Leo was keen to return, but it was difficult to drag Giles and Victor away. He kept on urging them to follow, but they were slow to heed his warning. As they approached the archway it suddenly closed and became a stone wall. He turned to face them. "Alas, we have delayed too long. You must remain here for the rest of your lives."

Edgar was getting fed up with doing nothing and went down the stairs to see what was going on. He hadn't been down and was surprised when there was nothing to be seen. He stood scratching his head, when the guide monk appeared.

"Oh, hello. What's going on?" he asked.

"Alas, your companions have delayed too long and are unable to return. My advice is to return to your home." He turned away and disappeared through the archway. Edgar hammered on the archway with both fists, but to no avail. He sat and thought for a while, then decided to take the monk's advice. He made his way back to the caravan only to find it was locked. He searched high and low, under the step, behind the gas bottle, and everywhere he thought there might be a spare key. Then he had a bright idea. There might be a key in the Land Rover. But he couldn't get into that either!

He was becoming frustrated at the prospect of not being able to get into either the caravan or the Land Rover. He returned to the monastery in despair and went down into the undercroft. He hammered on the wall where the archway had been and shouted hoping to bring the guide monk back, eventually screaming. Nothing. What could he do? He went back up to the chapel and retrieved a crowbar and, going back down, tried to chisel the archway with it. Suddenly he heard a noise like stones falling. Looking up he saw that the stone guarding the entrance was falling. It fell with a mighty crash, sealing the hatch to the chapel. He ran up the stairs and tried to move the stone. He remembered that when they opened it the first time it took all three of them to budge it. He was trapped. He sat down and wept. Eventually the paraffin in the lamp was exhausted, and he was alone in the dark, unable to escape.

# Best Served Cold

## Chapter 1

Frank had just left the pub with his girlfriend, Juliette, tagging along rather inattentively. He stumbled across the carpark and climbed into his car, fumbling with the keys and dropping them twice. Juliette got in and shut her coat in the door twice before settling into the seat. Her handbag fell to the floor, landing between her feet. Frank turned the radio on and leant across to kiss her. She wrapped her arms around his neck and willingly complied until he burped and filled the little car (and her mouth) with fumes of beer and pickles. She pushed him away with a laugh, grimaced, then returned to kissing. An hour later the pub closed, and the remaining customers flooded out into the carpark. Someone banged on the car roof, shouting, "Stop that, you disgusting creatures!" Frank got out and suggested they settle the disagreement with fists there and then, until the man's pals dragged him away. Not content, Frank shouted at the other customers, then the pub landlord came out and threatened to call the police. Frank still wasn't placated until Juliette pointed out that he might be over the limit and couldn't drive off if there were police around, and she was getting cold with the door open.

"Sorry, darling," he said, climbing back in. "But it's none of his business what we do in here. And it is getting a bit chilly. Come here and let me warm you up." Twenty minutes later there was a knock on the window at the passenger side. Juliette opened it cautiously. It was one of the bar staff.

"Sorry to spoil your fun, but the security man comes to lock the carpark in ten minutes, so if you're not out by then, you won't be able to get your car out until tomorrow lunchtime. Not wanting to cause a problem; just giving you fair warning."

Juliette thanked him and closed the window. "Come on," she said. "Let's find somewhere else. Somewhere a bit more private, and a bit warmer." Grumbling to himself, Frank settled into his seat and started the engine. He drove off through the carpark gates and headed away from the town centre.

"Are your folks in tonight?" he asked with a wink.

"Yeah. They're always in. Fancy having a life like that. Never going to the pub, never going to the pictures, never doing nothing except watch crap on the box." She folded her arms and put on a pretend grumpy face, which made him laugh.

"You mean never snogging with a gorgeous bloke like me?"

"I saw an old photo of Dad. When he was our age, he *was* gorgeous. And so was Mum. But not now. No wonder they don't snog no more." She laughed. Frank thought about it then he laughed too. They had pulled up at traffic lights and Frank was wondering which way to go, where there would be privacy and not too cold, when Juliette screamed. Frank looked at her. She was looking straight past him to the window on his side of the car. Frank looked out and saw a strange face. Quick as a flash he opened the door and jumped out. There was no-one there. He ran around the car to make sure the man wasn't hiding, but there was no-one there. There were no bushes or trees or walls anywhere nearby for the man to hide behind. He drew himself up to his full height and addressed the surroundings, summoning up all the volume he could manage.

103

"Come out, if you dare, you coward. I ain't scared of you. I don't want your type trying to scare my girlfriend, so if you ain't coming out, keep away." He might have used more colourful language than this, but no-one broke cover. He slowly climbed back in, all the while looking round for the man. They set off again, heading for the leisure centre carpark. It was free to get in, sheltered from the wind, and at this time of night, probably deserted, and if there was a security man, which Frank thought there wasn't, he was probably asleep in his little hut. This proved an ideal spot, and they stayed there for about an hour, until Juliette declared she needed to go home.

"I need a wee and I've got to go to work tomorrow, and …" She screamed again, looking through the car window. Frank looked round, and this time he saw it too. It was a man's face. Except it wasn't like a normal man's face. It was oval, pale green in colour, and had an evil grin. Assuming it was someone wearing a mask to scare them, he jumped out, only to find himself in the middle of a totally empty carpark. The man, if it was a man, had nowhere to hide, and hadn't had enough time to get away. He climbed back in and started the engine.

"I don't like this, darling," he said. "Let's get out of here. I'll take you home and see you tomorrow after work." He drove off. Half way along the bypass Juliette screamed again. Frank looked to his right, and there was the scary face, just as before, except this time they were doing about fifty miles per hour. He opened the window and it disappeared. Juliette was shaking, and he was inwardly, but didn't want to show it. He pulled into a lay-by and took her hand.

"Come on, darling, you'll be okay with me here. I won't let him hurt you." He put his arm round her shoulders and gave her a quick peck on the cheek. Tears were running down her face and she was trembling with fear. She squeezed his hand with one hand as she tried to wipe the tears away with the other, with a paper handkerchief from her handbag. When she had calmed down, they continued their journey to her home. "Do you want me to see you in?" he asked when they got there.

"Best not. You know Dad doesn't like you, and it's just a few yards to the front door. I'll get my key out ready. I'll be okay. I'll shout if there's anything, you know, strange."

They had a final kiss and she disappeared through the gap in the hedge. He waited until he heard the door close, then drove off. He thought about what had happened. The scary face in the pub carpark could be just some idiot having a laugh. And the idiot could have followed them to the leisure centre, but how he got away so quickly was a mystery. But the face, and it had been the same face on each occasion, the face appearing as they drove along at fifty miles per hour, well, how could that happen? He pulled back onto the bypass, looking around all the time, and only doing about thirty miles per hour, although he didn't know why. Then there it was again. He had glanced to his right, not for any reason other than to make sure he wasn't being followed or anything, and there it was in the window. The face. He opened the window and it disappeared. He closed the window and there it was again. He slammed the brakes on and got out. There was no sign of anything untoward. He got back in, wondering if getting out to face whatever it was had been a good idea. He hadn't come to any harm this time, but let's not take any chances next time. Five minutes later it happened again, but this time it was worse. He saw the face in his window and glanced across and saw it in the passenger side window, at the same time. He put his foot down and headed for home. Then he saw it in the front windscreen. It was directly in front of him, and he was having difficulty seeing the road. It was dancing about, smiling, as though it was taunting him. He decided it was too dangerous to carry on, but was it also too dangerous to stop?

Frank slowed to about ten miles per hour, and the faces remained at his windows, one at each side and one at the front. He pulled into a layby and wondered what to do. He couldn't carry on, as he couldn't see properly. But at this time of night the roads were empty, and he knew this road like the back of his hand, so he pulled away and put his foot down. He was up to eighty miles per hour in no time at all, but the faces were still there. He slammed the brakes on, almost putting himself through the windscreen had it not been for the seatbelt, but the faces remained. He had hoped they would be thrown off somehow. Opening the window, the face disappeared at that side. Closing it made it reappear. He got out of the car and couldn't see any of them. After making sure the three windows were clean, he was about to get back in when he realised there was a face peering out at him from within the car. It was smiling, almost laughing at him. Frank looked around and the road was deserted. He grabbed the door handle and yanked it open. The face disappeared. What should he do? It was starting to rain, and he hadn't brought a coat, as it was a fine, dry night when they came out. Yes, it was only water, but he'd had some chest problems recently and Juliette lectured him on keeping his chest warm every time he coughed. He closed the door and the face appeared in the car; he opened it and it disappeared. Enough messing about. He opened the door to get in and the face inside vanished, but the three outside reappeared. He hatched a plan. Opening the windows on both sides left only the face to the front. He put his head out of the window and drove very slowly. The rain was worse now and was hitting him in the face and getting in his eyes. Seeing clearly was difficult, but at least he could see a bit, and didn't have to look at that awful face jeering at him. He saw something on the road ahead and slowed down. It looked like a white sack (well, it used to be white) directly ahead in his lane, and partly obstructing the other lane. He stopped the car and got out. Dragging the sack onto the grass verge wasn't difficult. It wasn't heavy, but now and again the wind caught it and pulled it back onto the road. Eventually he got it settled under a hedge and got back in and set off for home. And the face from the windscreen had gone! Thank goodness for that! He had only gone a few yards when he noticed the wind had picked the sack up and it was up in the air in front of him, swirling about, and occasionally coming down on the front of the car before lifting up again. Exasperated, he stopped the car and got out. He grabbed the sack and angrily shoved it into the back seat. Ten minutes later Frank stopped at the traffic lights. He didn't remember seeing those lights there before, but he didn't want to risk being stopped by the police, as he was sure he would still be well over the limit. Glancing in the mirror, he saw the sack move. The light was still red; what should he do? Then the sack moved a bit more, and the face emerged, laughing at him. It was swaying about in the back seat. Frank panicked and pulled away. He put his foot down and reached seventy miles per hour in a very short time. The face was still there, still laughing, swaying about. It started to move towards him. He sped up further, not knowing what to do. He looked ahead and there was the face filling the front window. But it was still there in the mirror too. It was now so big he couldn't see where he was going and struck the kerb. The left side of the car left the road, and he travelled on two wheels for a while, then the left side came down on the grass verge. The car tipped over and tumbled over the barrier and the little stone wall behind it. The barrier was there for a reason. Behind the wall was a considerable drop down a steep bank into a field with a little stream flowing through it. The car tumbled down the bank and came to rest among some rocks in the stream at the bottom. Frank was knocked unconscious during the fall, and, as he had already undone his seatbelt at the traffic lights hoping for a quick escape to get away from the laughing face, his unconscious body bounced around and his head hit the steering wheel and the side window several times. When everything came to rest in the stream at the bottom, a trickle of blood made its way down Frank's face, dividing in two at the corner of his mouth where one continued to his chin while the other ran along his parted lips before running down the other side of his face. Blood dripped off his chin and soaked into his shirt, but he was unaware of this. In fact, he wasn't aware of anything.

The next morning a farmer telephoned the police to complain about a car in his field again and demanded to know why nothing was ever done about it, as this was the third one this year and it frightens the cows. When the local officer went to investigate Frank was already dead.

## Chapter 2

Titch wasn't very bright. He didn't understand why his pals called him 'Titch' as he was a big lad, approaching seven feet tall with broad shoulders and the strength of two men. Or possibly three. He worked on Dad's farm, not that Dad was there very often, as he seemed to spend a lot of time in prison. Titch saw to the cows and pigs and sheep, and his Uncle Fred popped in once a month to see if anything was ready for market, while Dad was away. In fact, Titch couldn't really remember the last time Dad took any livestock to market. Dad liked his drink, and every time he got out of prison he celebrated with several pints of beer and a couple of bottles of whisky. Usually he celebrated down the pub, The Country Gent being his favourite, and he would give them a serious amount of business before they threw him out and he would lie in the flower beds by the war memorial, snoring, and when awake, threatening anyone who disturbed him. This would bring the local police out, who would lock him up for the night. Upon release the next morning he would return to the scene and threaten everyone who looked the sort to complain about 'an honest man having a small glass or two in celebration'. Invariably this would lead to fisticuffs, and he would be up before the judge, and very soon back inside. Titch didn't really mind. Dad was violent when he was drunk, but he was violent when he was sober too, and Titch had ended up at the hospital many times with a broken arm or leg from Dad's use of the poker or walking stick or any other implement that came to hand. Dad suffered a broken leg a few years ago during a drunken brawl over who might or might not be cheating at dominos, and seriously injured members of the medical team when they tried to realign it, so it was now permanently twisted, and he couldn't run. This gave Titch an advantage. Despite being a bit overweight, stemming mainly from a poor diet as he couldn't read the instructions on packets, he could run quite quickly and had plenty of stamina, and had built a little hut in the woods on the hill across the stream from the farm. Dad knew he was hiding up there somewhere but could never follow him because of his deformed leg. Titch liked the animals and looked after them well. Uncle Fred would call the vet when a problem came along, saw to the utility bills and farm expenses, and gave Titch a weekly allowance to buy food and drink. Good old Uncle Fred; totally unlike Dad.

Titch had been out with his pals, which he did once a week. They were out every night, but Titch felt a responsibility to stay sober(ish) for the animals. He was tired, having had a difficult time with one of the sheep. Clover had wandered off and got stuck in a ditch. She was always doing things like that. Why couldn't she behave like the others? Anyway, Titch managed to get her out. It had been difficult, as she was by far the heaviest sheep in the flock, and it took all his strength, because she wasn't helping. It was almost as though she wanted to be back in the ditch. He chased her back to the others then managed to put up some temporary fencing to keep her out until he got a proper look in the daylight. It had been an exhausting day, and the first pint slipped down before the others were half way down theirs. After a pork pie and another pint Titch decided it was time to go. The others laughed, but he was tired after his escapade with Clover, so he finished another pie, downed the second pint, and made his way back to the farm. He trudged up the hill wearily and slipped the key into the lock. The door was already unlocked so he turned the handle and went in. There in the corner by the fireplace was Dad, sat in his favourite chair, with his pipe in his hand and a scowl on his face.

"Where you been?" he demanded aggressively. "I been here for more than an hour and I want something to eat."

"Oh, hello, Dad. I didn't know you was comin' out today."

"I didn't know neither, but here I am, so make me some dinner and pass my whisky bottle while I'm waitin'."

Titch passed the bottle. "I haven't got much in. I wasn't expecting you. I can do a sandwich. Will that do? Cheese or jam?"

"Sandwich?" roared Dad. "You haven't seen me for six months and all you can give me is a sandwich? You great useless oaf!" He reached for his walking stick, which was a stout implement made of oak, about four feet in length with a two inch diameter. Titch froze.

"No, Dad. Please Dad, no. I'm trying to make you something to eat. If I knew you was coming out, I'd have got you a pie or something." Dad swung the stick and caught Titch across the side of the head. He fell to the floor but was up onto his feet before Dad could manage another blow. "That's it, Dad. I've had enough. I'm off and I'm not coming back 'til you're back inside again." He left the house, slamming the door behind him, and made his way toward the bridge over the stream.

Dad got to his feet and stood at the door shaking his fist. "You come back here, you useless lump of shit! I wants something to eat, and I wants it now!"

"Get it yourself!" Titch shouted back at him, and turned away, heading for the bridge. Dad tried to run after him, but with his bad leg hindering him he could only manage a slow, one-sided trot. He continued the best he could, shouting, waving his stick and shaking his fist. Titch knew that with the constant pain from his bad leg, and the temper he was in, he'd soon give up the chase, go down to the village, have a pie in the pub, get blind drunk, and be back inside in a day or two. He pressed on in the gloom, which was turning to total darkness, as there weren't any streetlights up the track. He stopped to look back, but Dad was still in pursuit, so he set off at a trot again. Only one thing for it – his hut in the woods. He had a packet of biscuits, a bar of chocolate and a couple of tins of pop there, and that would do until he could get to the shop tomorrow. And there was a sleeping bag for when he needed to stay the night. He stopped and looked around again. Dad was still following. Titch was nearly at the bridge. That would stop Dad, because the track on the other side was for one thing much less even, and for another starting to go up hill. When he got to the bridge he turned once more, but Dad was still following him, cursing and swearing and threatening all manner of punishment. Titch set off to cross the bridge, then froze. There in front of him was Dad, on the other side of the bridge, stick in hand, snarling at him. He didn't know what to do. He turned to go back, but Dad was there too, having reached the bridge. Titch was cornered. He was stuck on the bridge with Dad on one side and Dad on the other. His slow brain struggled to get to grips with this. He knew there was only one Dad, but at the moment there were two, and they had him trapped. They were slowly walking toward him, sticks raised, faces distorted with rage, and he could tell they meant business. He only had one way out, and that was over the side. The stone parapet was only about a foot in height, so it wasn't difficult, and the drop was only about ten feet. He stepped onto the parapet and jumped, bending his knees as he hit the ground beneath, but it was uneven and covered in stones of varying sizes. His left ankle buckled under him as he landed and he fell to the side, hitting his head on a large stone, which made him see stars, and he couldn't tell which way was up for a moment. He called to Dad for help, but none came. He tried to get up but the pain in his ankle was excruciating and he fell over backwards, hitting his head again, and knocking himself unconscious. Blood oozed from the wound and ran down his neck and the side of his face. No-one ever came that way, as the bridge, the hill with the wood, and the track were all on Dad's land and Dad was fierce in defending it from trespassers. Dad never came that way, except when he was chasing Titch. No-one, not even Uncle Fred, had cause to walk along that track. His consciousness never returned.

## Chapter 3

Mick was on his way to the pub when his mobile rang. He stepped into the bus stop so that he could hear better. It was his friend, Jock.

"I'm locking up tomorrow night, so I can arrange things for you," Jock said. "I can disable the camera on the back fence, and leave the back door unlocked, and disconnect the sensor, like usual. Will that do?"

"That'll be great," Mick replied. "My van's off the road so I can only take what I can carry, but I've got a big back-pack, unless you can pop round to give me a hand."

"No chance. My car stands out a mile, and if they catch me that's the end to our little operation. No, we'll have to make do with what you can carry."

"Okay. But how come I'm doing all the heavy lifting?"

"I'm providing the inside knowledge. You couldn't do it without me."

"And you couldn't do it without me."

"Actually, yes, I could. I know two or three dodgy characters who would be more than happy to have a go at this. Contacts of my old man's contacts from when he was inside. So don't go getting ideas above your station; just be grateful for what I'm doing for you."

"Okay. You've made your point. What time can I start?"

"I finish at half six, then give it an hour to get dark and for the public to get out of the way. The security guys change over at about eight, so they'll not bother about anything so close to the end of the shift – they'll all want to be getting home for tea, lazy swine. So you needn't expect anybody interfering until quarter past eight, but make sure you're well gone by then. Or do you want to wait until your van's fixed and do it next week when it gets dark sooner?"

"No, it's a big job. I think it's totally knackered. I might need to get a new one but if I do that, I might not be able to use the same false plates – they're the right age and they belong to a van like mine. Different make of van means different plates."

"Okay. I'll come round at the weekend and we can see about shifting the stuff."

The next night saw Mick dressed all in black and hiding in the trees behind the industrial estate. Damn! They'd fixed the streetlight on the corner. It'd been off for a few weeks, and they chose now to repair it. So much for the council having no money! He had a big backpack, which was dark brown and blended in nicely with the trees. At half seven he crept out of his hiding place and cut a hole in the chain link fence big enough to get through with his backpack. It was further away from the door than he wanted, but at least it was in a shadow. He went through the hole on hands and knees and gave the back door a gentle push. It opened a fraction, but no bells or buzzers. He went in, dragging his bag behind him, and started filling it up with bottles of whisky, bottles of gin, bottles of vodka, pushing old socks between them to stop them rattling.

In Security Control Centre Rob and Pete had just settled down with steaming mugs of coffee and were going round the cameras in turn, when Pete stopped. "Look at this, Rob," he said to his colleague. "Camera three at Watson's Wine is off again. That's the third time this month. Our maintenance lads were there just the other week and couldn't find anything wrong with it."

"Has anybody put two and two together there? I hear they've been robbed two or three times recently."

Pete clicked on the radio. "Central Control to Unit 5 – do you read me?"

"Unit 5 here. Go ahead Central."

"Hi, Jonny. Are you anywhere near Dukes Industrial Estate?"

"I can be there in five minutes, Pete. What's up?"

"Nothing certain, just a hunch. One of their cameras has gone off for the third of fourth time this month. Pop round and have a look."

"Will do. I'll get back to you."

"Hey, Pete, look at this!" said Rob, pointing at the screen. The failed camera had sprung into life, and they saw a figure in the warehouse. Pete got back onto the radio to Jonny.

"There's someone in there, mate. Doesn't appear to be armed, and it looks like just one man. Rob'll contact the police then he'll get in touch with Mr Watson. When you get there have a scout round to see if there's anyone standing guard."

Five minutes later Jonny called back. "I'm here; I've been right round and there's no-one here. There's a hole in the fence by the back door and the door's ajar. I'm going in. Send the police round the back as well as the front. I'll leave the front door open."

Rob called the police with the update while Pete watched the screen intently. Jonny unlocked the front gate so the police could get in quickly, and went in through the front door, turning the alarm off on the way. He purposely made a noise and Mick heard it and froze. He wasn't expecting this. What should he do? Was there somewhere to hide? He spotted a door in the corner – that would do. Quietly opening it he went through. He'd never been in here before, and by the appearance, no-one else had been in for a while. He closed the door behind him, trying to be silent. In the room were two dozen or so huge wooden casks. There was a small window high up, and this admitted light from the streetlight. It wasn't much, but he could just about make out the words on one of the casks. It was wine from Spain. He clambered up and decided it made a good hiding place and settled between the two of the topmost casks. He waited, but no-one came. Good. He could stay there until all the fuss had died down then make an exit through the little window which was level with one of the top casks. He might have to leave his backpack behind, but it was better than being caught. He already had a record for minor burglaries, so next time could mean a custodial sentence, and he didn't want that.

Jonny had had a good look round and couldn't see any signs of forced entry, so he assumed the intruder had come in through the back door. He explained this to the police when they arrived. They explored every room with an unlocked door but found nothing. Just then Mr Watson arrived, and Jonny pointed out to him where the man had been seen. They made another search of that room but still found nothing.

"What's through that door, sir?" one of the officers asked, pointing to the door in the corner.

"Oh, that door hasn't been opened for months," Mr Watson answered. "That's where we keep wine maturing. It's due to be bottled in about six months. We only go in there once or twice a year."

The officer tried the door but found it to be locked. "Good," he said. "No need to waste time in there, then."

"That's right," declared Mr Watson. They chatted about the security measures until the forensic officers arrived to look for footprints, fingerprints, etc. "I'll be able to tell you what's missing, if anything, when the warehouse manager arrives in the morning." He made tea for the officers and Jonny filled in some forms then returned to his rounds. He got a call from Central to say the faulty camera was faulty again.

At about four in the morning Mick couldn't hear any sounds of activity, so he decided now was the time to make his escape, before it got light. He crawled along the top cask to the window but couldn't quite reach it. The gap between the cask and the wall was too much. He abandoned his bag of spirits for now and stretched out his arm. At full stretch he was about three inches short of the catch on the window. Not wanting to be there for ever, he overstretched and fell down the gap hitting his arms and legs on the way down. He landed on his head, and as he lay there unconscious a trickle of blood made its way down the side of his face. No-one came into that room for another five months.

## Chapter 4

Kenny wasn't an opportunist. Although many of his crimes made it look that way. No, when Kenny committed a crime, it was carefully planned. And this one was no exception. For six weeks he had been watching the little Post Office at the end of the parade of shops. Every Thursday two little old ladies would come along at six o'clock and withdraw cash. He didn't know how much. What mattered was that on the same day, half an hour later, when there was no-one about, absolutely no-one, a third little old lady would come along and make a withdrawal. The nights were getting lighter, but there was still no-one about. That morning at about three o'clock Kenny visited the Post Office armed with his catapult and after four near misses managed to take out the bulb in the streetlight. At six o'clock the two ladies arrived, tutted about the light not working, and did their usual business of taking their pension money out to see them through the week. Half an hour later it was still light enough to see, but only just, and the third lady came along. She too tutted at the broken light, considered the situation, and decided she could see well enough to proceed. She put her card in, took a slip of paper from her purse, and keyed in her PIN. She put the paper back into her purse before continuing, then made the request to withdraw cash, specified how much, retrieved her card and waited. After a few clicks and whirrs the cash emerged from the slot. She never got her hands on it. Quick as a flash Kenny unceremoniously shoulder charged her out of the way, grabbed the notes and fled. She fell to the ground, giving a quiet shriek as she went down, and held onto her handbag for dear life. Kenny never intended to hurt her but didn't care if he had. He had the desired cash in his hand and was running along the street as fast as his legs would take him. Yes, a successful operation; no-one about to see him except the old dear, but she was too shocked to take note of his face anyway. Ten minutes later a car pulled up and a middle-aged couple got out to help her to her feet and summon the police, and the ambulance just in case, although they both thought she was okay. Kenny was long gone by now. But an unmarked police car was following him. They had had a tip-off and were ready. There had been several thefts of newly extracted money in the little town, each one at a different cashpoint, but all at about the same time, and following the same method; and an unexpected lead had them sat in a car park in the shadows where no-one could tell if the car was occupied or empty.

After a while Kenny heard the siren and saw the blue lights. He turned left at the next junction and zig-zagged about, deviating from his route home. He couldn't shake them off and they were getting closer. He even tried running into the park, but the car followed him. Returning to the road where he could run more quickly, he took a sudden right turn and saw, directly ahead, the derelict pub, The Railway Flagman. He knew there was an open door at the back, so he took the opportunity to hide inside. He was quite fit, but even so he was breathless and in need of a rest. It took a few seconds for his eyes to adjust to the dark, then he saw a staircase immediately in front of him. He'd never been in this pub before, but he ran up the stairs and into one of the rooms, where he hid behind the bar counter and lay down, trying to breath silently. A couple of minutes later he heard the screech of tyres as the police car stopped. From where he lay, he could see the blue lights on the opposite wall, but they stopped very suddenly. The siren stopped too. The pub was totally silent. He daren't move, and lay there for more than half an hour, breathing very quietly.

The two plain-clothed officers had been following him for some time, gradually catching up. They made ground on the straight, but he could take corners more quickly than they could, so every deviation from the straight line helped him get away. They were just a few yards behind and had undone their seat belts ready for action, then Kenny took a sharp right-hand corner. They followed, then slammed the brakes on. In front of them was a brick wall, about ten yards away. Where did that come from? They got out and looked up at it, hands on hips it. It met the buildings at either side, and was too high, in excess of twenty feet, for Kenny to get over, there being nothing to give a handhold or foothold. The officers were perplexed.

"Where did he go?" asked one.
"He must've gone into a building," the other replied.
"But there's no doors. These are commercial places, and all the doors are on the front and back. And I don't remember seeing this wall here before either."
"That's right. I've been along this street before, and this wall's never been here."
They returned to their vehicle scratching their heads and reported back to base.

Kenny lay there in silence for some time. After a while he sat up and counted the money. Thirty pounds. That was a lot of running for just thirty pounds. He didn't usually need to run that far, or that fast, but hey, it was better than working for it. He stuffed it into his pocket and looked around. There was a bit of light from the streetlamp coming in through the window. Not enough to read by, but enough to see his way around. He got to his feet and explored the room further. A bottle of beer on the shelf behind the bar. He opened it, but it didn't smell good, so he left it. Nothing else, and nothing to eat either. What's this? A packet of nuts, but when he picked it up, he discovered the rats had got there first. Never mind. With thirty pounds in his pocket, he could get something on the way home. He was sure the old dear hadn't seen his face, so it wouldn't be a problem, just needed to change his clothes as soon as he got in. He made his way back to the stairs except they weren't there. After wandering about in the dark for half an hour he found the stairs, but he was sure they weren't the ones he came up. Never mind. These would do. He set off down, slowly in the near total darkness as the room with the window was on the other side, and felt the stair move beneath him. He grasped the handrail firmly in both hands and crept down one stair at a time. Suddenly the stairs gave way and he found himself hanging onto the handrail and swinging in open space. He tried to get a foothold on what was left of the edge of the stair, but that crumbled as soon as he put any weight on it. Then he heard a creaking sound; the handrail was beginning to move. The more he struggled the more it creaked and fell over until it collapsed, and he plummeted down, landing rather badly on a piece of broken timber, its sharp point going through his side, impaling him about three feet above the floor. He felt something wet on his face and realised he had hit his head on something on the way down. It was just a trickle, but who knows, it could get worse. But to be honest that was the least of his worries at the moment. He tried to free himself, but it was too painful. He tried shouting. That too was painful and proved fruitless, but it was his only option. He shouted until he had no energy left. Surely some-one would come in sooner or later. He stayed quiet until daylight shone a faint beam of light through a small window. He shouted again and again, but no-one came. His blood dripped onto the floor, forming a little pool. Rats came to lick it up – an early Christmas dinner for them.

Six weeks later a building firm bought the place and sent a demolition team in. They found Kenny, still impaled on the spike of wood, but the rats had had their fill.

## Chapter 5

Joseph was a quiet lad. He had left home as soon as he could support himself, as his parents both had problems with the drink, and weren't slow to take his money to pay for it, or 'borrow' his belongings to sell down the pub. They had done nothing to encourage him at school, and never supported him in any of his interests or hobbies. He felt he owed them nothing and proved this by leaving messages on their answerphones for their birthdays and Christmas, and never got replies. He lived his solitary life quite contentedly. He had a steady, if sometimes tedious, job in the office at a local firm, which paid him enough to meet his outgoings with a little bit left over. His job was to produce the documentation for overseas shipments. This was sometimes too simple, and at other times a bit complicated, depending on what was being shipped and where to. But he was content. He spent his spare time birdwatching in the summer and listening to the radio in the winter, with a weekly visit to the gym to keep himself fit.

One day he was in his favourite spot, under a tree in a meadow just outside town, with a view of several groups of trees. He had some decent binoculars and sat watching the birds coming and going. Eggs had recently hatched so there was plenty of activity. He remained there for a while, trying to be silent, with his packet of sandwiches and flask of coffee, watching them and making sketches in his notebook, pausing for an occasional bite to eat or sip of coffee. He was distracted by movement on his left, some way off, which he just caught out of the corner of his eye. It was those idiots from the pub. Four young men he had been at school with, not his type at all, and when they got together, usually up to no good. They were laughing and pointing as they strolled across the meadow, making towards him. They stood around him, hands on hips, trying to look menacing, and succeeding.

"Hello, Joseph," said Kenny. "Haven't seen you for a while. Are you still boring?"

"Yes, you were boring at school," chimed in Mick. "So why are you out here? No pals, no girlfriend, nothing to do. Is it dreadful being this boring?"

"I'm okay with it," Joseph replied through gritted teeth. "I'm happy with my life. Decent job, a few hobbies to fill my time."

"What's this?" Frank asked, snatching up Joseph's notebook. "Birds? What's so special about them?"

"They're interesting to watch, beautiful to look at and draw. Part of nature. Give it back, please." Frank threw it away. Joseph got up to retrieve it.

"Sort him out, Titch," Kenny barked. Titch looked confused.

"What? What do you mean? What's he done?"

"Don't let him get it. He's being disrespectful." Titch didn't understand, but he stood in front of Joseph.

"You're a decent bloke at heart, Titch," Joseph said, looking Titch in the eye. "When are you going to understand that you're better than these three? Why do you always do what they tell you without thinking about it? Why not question their instructions now and again?"

"He's calling you stupid, mate," said Mick. "I wouldn't stand for that if I was you. Show him who's boss." Titch threw a punch at Joseph. It wasn't very hard, but it caught him squarely in the stomach and was enough to make him double up. "Give him a bit more, Titch. Just remember, you're our pal, and he's making fun of you, and he'll start on us soon. Best stop it before it starts. This is what to do." Mick punched Joseph firmly on the nose, which started to bleed. Joseph was knocked back a couple of steps while they all laughed. He struck back, landing a punch on Mick's jaw, which put him off balance, so Joseph threw another, this time knocking him to the ground. His fists flew somewhat at random at Kenny and Frank, catching them both twice, but without any force. Seeing his pals suffering, Titch waded in, and his next punch put Joseph on the floor. He stood and watched while the other three took their revenge on the unconscious man. Titch was worried.

"Look! I've killed him!" he shouted, panic on his face. "I've killed him! They'll lock me up! They locked Dad up for a lot less than this!" Titch was starting to get carried away in his panic, so the other three grabbed him and pulled him to the ground.

"Look, mate," said Frank. "Calm down. He's probably not dead. And if he is, it ain't a problem. We all saw you hit him in self-defence. But anyway, if he's dead we'll just hide the body where nobody can find it until after the wolves have eaten him and then they won't know who he was or how he died. Just don't panic."

"Wolves? There's no wolves around here! I'd know if there was 'cos they'd get my sheep." Titch said in disbelief. Kenny shook his head looking crossly at Frank.

"No, mate, there's no *wild* wolves," Kenny said firmly. "But every now and then they escapes from the zoo and wanders round until they gets caught again. There's other farms closer to the zoo, and them's the ones that loses sheep. You've seen it in the paper. Sheep go missing. Happens all the time."

"I thought that was rustlers."

"No, mate. That's what they say so folk won't worry about the wolves. It happens all the time, but not near here. When was the last time you or your neighbours lost sheep?" Titch stood quietly, counting on his fingers.

"I never lost any. Old Mr Reed, he lost a few, but that was about twelve years ago."

"There you are. They gets out of the zoo, they kills a few sheep nearby, then they gets caught, then they gets locked up again. Reed's farm is near the zoo; yours isn't." Titch stood pondering for a while then he spoke again.

"But if there ain't no wolves to get my sheep, that means there ain't no wolves to eat poor Joseph." He looked round at their puzzled faces. Frank was the first to break the silence, which was starting to be uncomfortable.

"No, Titch, mate, you ain't understanding. The wolves might not get him, but other things will. There's badgers and other animals round here – they'll eat him. And the rooks and crows, you know there's plenty of them, they'll clean up after the others are finished."

"But Frank said there was wolves. Is he stupid?" Frank's face took on an angry expression and he stepped forward, about to grab Titch's jacket, until Kenny stepped in. He got between them and reversed into Frank, pushing him into Mick's arms.

"Shut up, you idiot," Mick growled in a whisper into Frank's ear.

"Titch, mate," Kenny said, putting his arm onto Titch's mighty shoulder. "Frank's a clever guy, but every now and then he can be stupid." Frank tried to break free from Mick's hold, but Kenny saw this out of the corner of his eye and turned suddenly, elbowing Frank firmly in the stomach. "Oh, sorry mate, did I bump you? So you see, Titch, all we need to do is move the body to somewhere it won't be discovered, and we can forget about this unfortunate incident. Okay?"

"When you puts it like that, I'll do what you tells me 'cause you knows what's what. You ain't stupid, not like Frank." Frank was still cross, but Mick and Kenny were trying not to laugh. Frank tried to break free again and was about to speak, but Kenny stamped on Frank's foot to shut him up.

"Come on, guys let's hide the body. Titch, you're the strongest. Pick him up." Titch slung Joseph over his shoulder, fireman's lift style, and followed the others.

"There's a little gully in the corner of the meadow," said Mick. "No-one would find him there for weeks. Months even. Can't be seen from the road."

"How d'you know about that? What you been doing up this way?" asked Kenny.

"You know me," said Mick with a smug expression and a wink. "Sometimes I needs to know where to hide." The other two laughed.

When they reached the gully they all paused at the top.

"There you go, Titch," said Kenny. "Throw him in." Titch paused.

"Shouldn't we say a few words?" Titch asked.

"What?" said Frank, surprised. "What you talking about?"

"Well, when I buries one of my sheep dogs, I always says a few words. You know, like a prayer, sort of."

"But your sheep dogs is useful. This is Joseph. Never useful to any of us. I never liked the guy anyway. Always getting stuff right at school. Always made out he was better than us. No, just throw him in. Make sure he goes into the water. As it flows away it might attract other vermin to eat his guts." Titch thought about this for a moment, then threw Joseph's body into the gully. Joseph's head hit a rock as it landed, and blood oozed out, running down his face and mingling with the water. As they turned to go Titch stopped, bowed his head and mumbled a 'few words' to salve his conscience. They stopped off at the pub for a pint and a pie before Titch, unsettled by all this, went back to work.

## Chapter 6

I tried to get up, but it hurt too much. It hurt just to turn my head. I had a throbbing pain in the back of my head and I could feel something warm trickling down my face. Blood, I suppose. It hurt to move my arms, too, and my legs refused to do anything. The pain in my head was getting worse, and eventually I couldn't bear it any longer, so I shut my eyes and I suppose I passed out.

About an hour later, judging by the sun, I awoke. The pain had gone, so I got to my feet. I looked around me, and there, on the ground, was my body, with blood and water easing past it, making its way to the stream near Titch's farm. I suppose I must be dead. That was a bit unexpected, but we all have to go some time or other. I flexed my arms and legs, and everything appeared to be working okay. Climbing out of the gully, I realised that the ground I was standing on was a bit unstable. In fact, I wasn't really standing on anything, and I hadn't really climbed out. All I had to do was 'will' myself along, and along I went. But I went through the motions of moving legs and arms as though I was walking, just to keep a bit of mental stability. This part of the meadow was quite flat, but I soon noticed that when I went uphill or downhill I had to think a bit harder to stop myself 'sinking' into the ground, or 'floating up' off it. Not that it really mattered all that much, but as I said earlier, it helped with mental stability.

On the way home I saw some children throwing stones up into a tree. I went close to see what they were doing, and noticed they were trying to hit a nest, which appeared to have some baby birds in it. Every time they threw a stone the mother bird would fly off, then return a few moments later to tend to her young. This made me cross, and I shouted at the children to stop it. They hadn't noticed me up to that point, but now they shrieked and ran off.

Arriving at my flat, taking the stairs in a single bound was much easier than thinking about each individual stair. I pulled the key out of my pocket, but when I tried to put it in the lock I just fell through the door. I 'sat' in my armchair and planned my revenge. I thought about the children and got up to look in the mirror. Nothing. No reflection. I thought about things to make myself angry, and suddenly there I was, semi-transparent, but there in the mirror, looking a bit ghostly. I practiced this a few times and decided it would be part of my revenge. But could I alter my appearance? No, but I noticed the local paper, 'The Mercury', on the coffee table, and the bottom corner showed an advert for the cinema – 'Aliens from Outer Space' – with a picture of a horrible face, pale green and almost circular. I stared at it for a few moments then went back to the mirror and thought about the face quite intently. My own face appeared at first, then it changed and began to resemble the alien. Again, lots of practice needed. After about an hour of practice I could make myself visible without being angry and could impose the alien face on mine. And I could make one image hang in the air while causing another image (or indeed another copy of the same image) to appear somewhere else.

The next few weeks were spent following my murderers around, learning their customs and habits. One evening I visited their local, sat down at their table, and made myself appear. Never before had I heard such shrieks from grown men. They jumped up knocking the table over, then fled the pub. Most of the regulars hadn't seen me and laughed heartily. But one or two *had* seen me and were more than just a bit disturbed. I decided not to do that again, as most of the people there were decent types, and I didn't want to scare them. But when I had enough information, I went after Frank. Sunday night was his most regular night out with his girlfriend, Juliette. They always went to the same pub, The Blacksmith's Arms, and they tended to leave at about the same time every week. Sure enough, there they were, snogging in the car park, and being turfed out by the landlord. I followed the car for about half a mile, then appeared at the window when they stopped at the traffic lights. This scared them, and they took off. I followed them and did it again. After he had taken Juliette home, I put in another appearance, then started showing off by appearing in two places at once, then three. Frank was getting desperate, so I moved into the car. That business with the white sack was just a coincidence, but it helped. Anyway, the little car rolled down the bank and Frank's head made contact with the steering wheel and windows several times before it stopped. I don't know if he survived or not, but I know the bottom of the bank was a desolate place, so if he did survive the fall, he would be in a lot of pain for quite a while.

For Titch I needed a bit of preparation earlier in the month. His dad wasn't due out of prison for a few weeks, but I found out where he was and paid him a visit. I didn't appear to him, but concentrated on what he looked like when he was standing, walking and shaking his fist, which he seemed to do a lot of. After some practice I could appear in his form, and practiced a bit in the prison, which confused some of the wardens. After a bit of fine tuning, I could do an impression that no-one could tell from the real thing. I knew when he was coming out, and I knew he hadn't told Titch. This was ideal. On the appointed day I sat in the farmhouse and waited. I heard the sound of the key trying to make its way into the lock. He struggled to manage that, because he hadn't had a drink for a few months, but eventually he got in. Leaning on his stick, the first thing he did was grab the whisky bottle, which didn't have much in, and drained it. He threw himself into the armchair by the fire and muttered and grumbled, inspecting the whisky bottle in case it had refilled itself, which it hadn't. I could have had some fun if I'd been prepared, but I wasn't. After a while Titch came in. The smile disappeared when he saw his dad. After some sharp words from Dad and a plea for patience from Titch, Titch ran out. Dad followed but was no sooner out of the farmhouse when he stumbled and fell, and the chase came to an end. But Titch didn't notice. He headed for the stream where he stopped and turned and saw dad unexpectedly close. Of course, it wasn't his father; it was me. I was good enough to fool him, and when he started to cross the bridge, there I was again, this time in front of him. He looked back, saw me again, and in a state of panic, leapt off the bridge into the stream. I heard his cry as he landed and knew I had done enough. No-one ever came that way, as the old man was one to strike first with his walking stick then ask questions afterwards.

 Poor Titch. The other three always used him for entertainment, and the locals in the pub joined in. There was always someone would point to some large object and call out, "I'll buy you a pint if you can lift this over your head!" and someone else would follow up with, "And I'll buy you a pie to go with it if you can do it with one hand!" and Titch was happy to oblige. He didn't know the difference between cheering and jeering, laughing with and laughing at. He was always kind to his animals. He might have had a better life without his drunken father and his three dodgy pals. In a way I felt sorry for him, but when all's said and done, he had contributed more to my demise than any on the others.

Mick was always up to something, so I didn't have to wait long for an opportunity. I needed more preparation for his demise, as I needed to learn new skills. I needed to be able to manipulate material things – something I hadn't needed so far. That took a lot of practice, and I mean a lot! After lots of really hard concentration I could move things with my mind. I went through the motions of using my hands just to make it easier to concentrate, but it was all done with my mind. Sliding something across the floor became quite easy after a while, but turning things such as a door knob or a key took more effort. Electrical and electronic devices seemed to be fighting back, but I succeeded, although I needed to rest for a few moments to stop the dizziness which always ensued. After about three weeks of practicing, I felt I was up to it. When Mick got the phone call from his pal, Jock, it wasn't Jock – it was me. I turned off the camera and the door sensor, leaving the door unlocked, and made the streetlamp work; it wasn't repaired – I just made it give light. Then I made the camera work again so the guys in the control room could see Mick. And when their man arrived, I got inside Mick's head and made him spot the door in the corner. Next came the difficult part – really difficult. I managed to unlock the door without using the key and lock it again after Mick had gone through. After that I needed a rest, so I went back to my flat, which wasn't far away, and rested. When I say 'rested' all I mean is, I stopped thinking for a while, perhaps an hour or two, to recharge the batteries, as it were. My work done on Mick, I never thought about him again.

Kenny was a nasty piece of work. He took what he wanted and didn't care about hurting whoever got in his way. He was the cleverest of the four and planned his jobs. I saw him staking out the little Post Office and watching for potential victims. Kenny seemed to be interested in little old ladies, especially those who turned up alone, as they would offer the least resistance. There were three who always came on Thursdays, and Kenny took an interest in these, making notes in his little book. I went along to the police station and got inside the desk officer's head. He wrote down what I had to 'say' and entered it all into the computer. CID sent their men along to sit and wait. They sent a car along on the Thursday. Nothing happened, so they sent along another on the following Thursday, with a little prompting by me. This time it all happened. Kenny knocked the old dear over and grabbed her dosh, then legged it around the corner and off into the distance. The car followed and was catching him up, but he was quick and able to change direction sharply. He led them a merry chase for a while. Then he turned into Factory Road. This was ideal! The walls were blank on both sides; no houses or doors – just the side walls of factories. There were houses further along and a pub at the end, but I didn't let them get that far. I had concentrated on a brick wall earlier in the day and was able to make one appear just behind him. The police officers were totally flummoxed, as they knew the area and hadn't seen a wall there before. Kenny was too quick to notice, but he saw the pub, and I got into his head and made him head for it. In he went by the back door, up the stairs, and lay on the floor trying to get his breath back. He explored, but found nothing to eat or drink, so when he decided he had been there long enough for the police to give up, he made his way back to the stairs. Except he didn't find them. I drove him round in circles for a while, then guided him to different stairs. These were a bit rickety, and as he slowly made his way down, I managed to push him off balance, and as he grabbed the handrail it gave way. The stairs collapsed and down he went. I heard his cry of pain and looked over the edge to see him impaled on a piece of wood. That was good enough for me.

I'd had an exhausting time with Mick and Kenny. Frank and Titch had been much easier, but I had succeeded. Four out of four. I made my way home wondering what to do next. I lay on my bed and switched off. A few days later I felt a sudden urge to get up. I found myself drifting towards the gully where I met my end. I tried to change direction, but I couldn't. After a few seconds (well, that's what it seemed like to me) I was back at the gully. There in the bottom of the gully lay my body. Bits had been eaten, which was quite off-putting, but everything was now out of my control. I drifted down the side and lay down on top of my body. I realised what was happening – my revenge was complete; my murderers were dead. I felt my spirit being absorbed into my corpse, and an easiness swept over me. I could rest in peace. In fact, I had no choice. Resting in peace was the only thing I *could* do. Pity about Titch, but the choice was his.

# The Hospitals

## Chapter 1

Staff Nurse Julia was updating the patients' records on the computer while the other two chatted noisily about what they might do next time they had a night off.

"Keep the noise down a bit, girls," complained Julia. "I'm trying to work over here. If you've got nothing to do, Marian, you can check that cupboard for bandages and stuff – you know where supplies are kept downstairs. And you, Lorraine, you can, well," Pause. "You can make us a coffee. Do you think you can do that?"

"I can do that, boss. How do you like it?"

"You've made me coffee every night this week. Milk with no sugar. And don't call me 'boss'."

"Okay, boss. Sorry, I mean Julia. And I forgot what you had last night. I'll try to remember that. How do you want yours, Marian?"

"Black without sugar, please. And without milk too." Marian answered, trying not to laugh. Lorraine strutted off to the rest room at the other end of the ward, swinging her hips as she went. Halfway along she stopped.

"No, Mr Robson, you're supposed to be in bed. Go back to your bed and try to get some sleep."

"Who's she talking to?" Julia asked Marian. "Mr Robson can't get out of bed – he's in a coma."

Marian leant out into the corridor. "Looks like Mr Robson. But it can't be." She stopped what she was doing and went along to Mr Robson's bed, as the figure walking along the corridor had disappeared. She came running back. "Julia, I think Mr Robson's dead! Will you come and check please?"

Julia paused her screen and went along at a brisk walk. She examined Mr Robson while Marian checked the connections on the equipment. "Yes, he's gone," she answered after feeling for his pulse and listening for his breathing. She pushed the machine away. "I'm starting CPR. Give the duty doctor a call. He should be just one floor away by now." She administered CPR while Marian ran back to the nursing station to call the doctor. A few moments later he came running in and examined the patient. They worked on him for several minutes, but eventually the doctor shook his head.

"It's no use, Staff," he said gravely. "He's gone. Let's have a look at his notes to see about informing his family." They walked back to the nursing station just as Lorraine arrived with a tray of coffee cups.

"Oh, hello, Doc. If I'd known you were here I'd have brought you one too."

"Lorraine, Mr Robson's dead," said Julia.

"Dead? Mr Robson? But he can't be. I just saw him walking along here a few minutes ago. When did this happen?"

The doctor looked at Julia. "No, he can't have been. Look, the bedding hasn't been disturbed, other than what we did to try to revive him. You must have been mistaken."

Lorraine burst into tears. "But I did! I saw him walking along, and I told him to get back to bed. They heard me!" She pointed accusingly at the other two nurses. "Everybody thinks I'm stupid, but I know what I saw!"

Marian put her arm around Lorraine's shaking shoulders. "Actually, I saw him too," she said. "At least, it looked like him, and none of the patients in this part of the ward is anywhere near as tall as him. The man I saw couldn't have been anyone else." At this Lorraine straightened up and dried her eyes. She clasped Marian's hand.

"Thank-you, Marian. I did see him, didn't I?"

"I saw the same as you. Now sit down and drink your coffee." Julia retrieved Mr Robson's file on the computer while the doctor waited patiently. Lorraine declared her coffee was too hot to drink, so Marian sent her to get a coffee for the doctor. "Lorraine's a bit scatty, and not dreadfully bright, but she *is* reliable. Very reliable. If she says she saw him, she saw him. And I saw him too," she said to the doctor, as soon as the young nurse was out of earshot. He nodded.

"I understand what you're saying, but there's no way that man has been out of bed recently," he said. "Just look at the state of the bedding – the bottom half is pretty much undisturbed."

"I have his records here," Julia announced. "His family don't want to be disturbed during the night," she said. "His son and daughter-in-law are both in poor health, and their son has issues – mental health or learning disabilities or something. I'll start the paperwork and we can finish the other procedures tomorrow morning. I know it's a bit irregular, but it isn't every day someone doesn't want to know their father's died."

By now Lorraine had returned with coffee for the doctor. He thanked her and asked her to sit down.

"You seem a bit shaky," he said, gently. "Is this the first time you've seen someone die?"

Lorraine shook her head. "No, I've seen plenty of dead people, but this is the first time I've seen one wandering about."

The doctor glanced at Marian. "And you? What did *you* see?"

Marian shrugged her shoulders. "I saw the same as Lorraine. I saw a tall man walking along the corridor, a bit unsteady on his feet, and it did look like Mr Robson. But he's been in a coma for a while, so I was surprised. In fact, I didn't believe my own eyes at first, but when I came to help him back to bed, well, he was already in bed, and he seemed pretty dead, so I called for Julia. But there wasn't anyone else out of bed, so I don't understand, really."

He shook his head again and stood up. After thanking them, he turned to Julia. "Give the mortuary a ring. I'll give you a hand getting things started, then I'll pop along to the other wards to make sure there's nothing urgent going on. If I get time, I'll come back for the handover to the morning shift."

"Thanks, Bob. There's no reply from the mortuary. I'll try again later," she sighed, looking stressed. He gave her a friendly pat on the shoulder and smiled sympathetically.

"Well, if there's no joy from the mortuary, we need to get him moved to a side room temporarily."

The next morning Bob came to the ward to be greeted by the duty doctor for the morning.

"What's going on, Bob?" she asked. Bob looked puzzled.

"What do you mean, Jamila?" he replied.

"Why did you put Mr Robson into this side room and upset the nurses?"

"Well, I suggested they put him in here because he's dead, until the mortuary staff were available this morning. Staff tried to get them last night but there wasn't an answer, which I found a bit disturbing. People do sometimes die in the night."

"Dead? No, he isn't. He's in the same condition he was in when I first examined him three weeks ago. Walk this way." He followed her into the side ward. She stood by the bed, hands on hips, while he examined Mr Robson.

"I don't believe this," he said. "Good job you reconnected his tubes and wires, but he was definitely dead at three this morning."

"Yes, what did you think you were doing disconnecting the life support of an elderly man in a coma?"

"No, you don't understand. At three this morning HE WAS DEAD! I did all the normal checks, which Staff had already done, and there was no doubt about it. Mr Robson had passed away."

## Chapter 2

That night Julia, Marion and Lorraine were on duty together again. The didn't speak about the events of the previous night, as none of them was sure what had happened. The atmosphere was subdued, and nothing of note was taking place on the ward.

"Shall I get teas and coffees?" Lorraine volunteered.

"Yes, please!" chorused the other two. Off she went. Marian had finished checking stocks of bandages etc, and strolled down the ward while Julia did some updating on the computer. She suddenly reappeared at the nurse station, walking in backwards quite quickly and stopping so she could see along the corridor.

"Staff, you've got to see this. I'm not taking my eyes off it until you've seen it and can tell me I'm not going mad." Julia got to her feet and stood next to Marian looking along the corridor. "Is that who I think it is?" she whispered.

"Well, it can't be, but it does look like Mr Robson."

"Yes, I saw him come out of his side room and slowly walk away. What do we do? Do we try to stop him?"

"Have to, really. Let's follow him quietly and try to catch him up."

They followed the old man, getting quicker and quicker, but not gaining any ground on him, even though he didn't seem to be speeding up. He went through the doors at the end of the corridor, and they ran to follow. There was no sign of him. Julia ran back to the nursing station and telephoned security. "One of our patients is trying to escape. He's very sick and mustn't be allowed out. He's about six feet six, about ninety years old, and wearing light blue pyjamas. We were trying to catch him but he left us behind, somehow."

"Okay, we'll keep an eye out and stop him if he comes this way. We'll let the guys on the other doors know too."

An hour later Marian and Lorraine were going round doing obs and were about to pass Mr Robson's room when Lorraine let out a little gasp. "Look in there! There's somebody in his bed!"

Marian went in, then called to Lorraine. "It's Mr Robson, but he looks dead; he's got no pulse. Go and get Staff."

Julia came running and checked Mr Robson's pulse and breathing. She started CPR and called to Marian, "Get the duty doctor! Be quick!" A few moments later the duty doctor arrived, breathless. It was Bob again.

"Not him again!" he gasped as he helped Julia. After a while they stopped. "No, he's dead. We've failed to revive him, just like we failed to revive him last night."

"But we saw him making off," said Julia. "Marian and I both saw him. We tried to follow him, but he was too fast."

"So how did he get back here?" asked Bob.

Julia and Marian glanced at each other and shrugged their shoulders. "Haven't a clue," said Julia. "Probably the same way he got back last night."

"Well, I'm not moving until we get another doctor. I got a really harsh email about last night. Jamila really dropped me in it, although if it had been the other way round, I probably would have done the same. Can one of you phone J Block and ask the duty doctor there to come over? I think they have two on duty tonight because of the numbers of patients." Julia returned to the nursing station and was about to make the call when the phone rang.

"I demand an explanation!" shouted an angry voice. "What's going on? Just what do you think you're doing? If he dies it will be your fault and I'll make sure you are on the front pages of the Sunday papers. Now get an ambulance here now and take him back to hospital and do it now and get some help for my son. He's beside himself, not knowing if Granddad's going to live or die."

When he paused for breath Julia spoke, "Sorry, but I don't know who you are. What is your name, please?"

"Don't you know? Can't you work it out? You're obviously not aware of what's going on on your ward. I'm Derek Robson – Raymond Robson's son. You know, the sick old man that you've sent home in the middle of the night wearing nothing but a flimsy pair of pyjamas. Now get this sorted out immediately, and I mean immediately, or I'll call the police and have you arrested."

"Slow down a bit, Mr Robson. Your father is here in the hospital. I was in his room just a few minutes ago."

"Don't give me crap like that. He was in my son's bedroom fifteen minutes ago, just like he was last night."

"Can you bring him to the phone, please?"

"No, I can't. I put a dressing gown round his shoulders to keep him warm and put him in the car to bring him back, then he disappeared."

After a short silence Julia spoke again. "So he isn't in your son's bedroom?"

"Well, no."

"And he isn't in your car?"

"No."

"Is he anywhere else in your house?"

"I don't know. I don't think so. But he was."

"So you've lost your father in the middle of the night. Is that what has happened?"

"Well, sort of, but what was he doing here in the first place? He's not well enough to be out by himself, especially at this time of night. We were told he was in some sort of a coma and not to visit because he wouldn't know us, but he knew my son last night."

"I think you'll find he isn't out at the moment. He's in the hospital. He's on my ward. And he was last night too. I'm not sending anyone to collect a patient who isn't there. Now I have important work to do. If you want to complain, not that there's anything to complain about, the complaints department will be open tomorrow morning at nine o'clock. Thank-you, Mr Robson. Goodbye." She slammed the phone down and burst into tears. Marian came in, knelt beside her, and put a comforting arm around her shoulders.

"What's this about, Julia?" she asked gently.

"I've just had Mr Robson's son on the phone accusing us of not taking care of his dad. He says he was in their house twenty minutes ago. Obviously, he can't have been because he was here. What's going on, Marian?"

Marian shook her head slowly while she wiped Julia's tears. "I don't know, Julia. I've sent Lorraine to make coffee for the doctors and us. This doesn't make sense. Dr Solomon came over from children's and he agrees that Mr Robson is dead. Bob's already getting grief about the incident last night so he wanted an independent witness in case there's a repetition of last night's goings on."

## Chapter 3

Julia was invited into Matron's office where a man in a business suit was already seated. Matron introduced him.

"This is Mr Hodges, from the Complaints Department," she said, with a grim expression. "He will tell you the nature of the complaint then we will decide together the best way to handle it."

"Please call me Tim," he said, getting up to shake hands. "And don't be alarmed, I'm on your side. Ninety per cent of complaints are without foundation and we go out of our way to exonerate our staff. This one seems a bit off the planet, but we'll do what we can to get it resolved quickly. Please tell me, in your own words, what happened, as best as you can recall."

He listened intently while Julia told him the whole story from her point of view. He took notes as she was speaking and kept referring to a document he had taken from the folder in front of him. At some points Julia appeared confused, and her lip trembled, but Matron put her hand on Julia's arm and smiled comfortingly. When she had finished he looked up and smiled.

"Thank-you, Julia. That is exactly what you said in your written report. From what you have just told me, in my opinion you have done nothing wrong. There are some, well, I'm not sure how to describe them, perhaps I'll call them 'irregularities' for now. I'll now tell you what Mr Robson, Mr Derek Robson, that is, told us when he registered his complaint. Now some of this sounds strange too, just as some of your report was strange, but my job is to put the two together and decide who, if anyone, is not telling the truth, and then decide if there is an element of malice or negligence about any untruths. Let's begin on Wednesday evening last week. That makes it the tenth of April. Mr Robson first noticed that his son, whose name I am not permitted to give at this point, awoke during the night at about three o'clock – that actually makes it the eleventh of April, and was heard speaking to someone. Now when he says 'awoke' he admits he is assuming that, as neither he nor his wife went to investigate until some minutes later, by which time the boy had stopped speaking. This introduces the first strange point – the boy has severe learning difficulties and can't string a sentence together. He hasn't said more than three words at a time in the whole of his life. He is twelve and goes to a special school for children with his condition, which I can't disclose at present for GDPR reasons – I'm sure you understand. But here he was talking almost fluently in the middle of the night. The next morning, they asked him about it and eventually he got them to understand he was talking to his grandfather who had been sitting on the bottom of his bed. Of course, grandfather was in hospital at the time, so they assumed, understandably, the boy had had a dream. They weren't surprised, as the boy and grandfather had been close until Mr Robson Snr's health took a turn for the worse. But they were surprised at the boy's fluency. Do you wish to comment before I go on?"

"Well, yes," said Julia. "Three o'clock was around the time Lorraine saw Mr Robson out of bed and walking along the corridor. She called out to him to get back to bed. Marian went along to investigate, because she knew it couldn't possibly be Mr Robson. Don't know if it's at all relevant, or just a coincidence."

"Right. I've made a note of that. Shall I go on?" Julia nodded. "Okay. About the same time the next night, so that's about three o'clock on the Friday morning, they heard the boy talking again, so Mrs Robson got up and went into his room and found Mr Robson Snr sat on the bottom of the bed, and he was having a conversation with the boy, who was sat up in bed, and appeared to be wide awake. She went back and woke her husband, who also came to the child's room. He was cross and wrapped a dressing gown round the man's shoulders and sat him in an armchair while he put some shoes on to drive the car. He helped his father into the car, but by the time he had got round to the other side of the car the father had disappeared. He looked around but there were no signs of him, and nowhere he could hide either. That's when he telephoned you. What he says he said to you agrees, almost word for word, with your version of the conversation, so there is no conflict there. Mrs Robson had been comforting the boy, who was upset at his grandfather being taken away, but he suddenly became calm, and she was able to put him back to bed." He put down his pen and had a sip of his tea, as though waiting for Julia to speak.

"Do you want to have a few minutes to get some fresh air?" Matron asked Julia, who was visibly upset. Julia nodded and left the room. Five minutes later she returned looking refreshed.

"Sorry about that," she said. "Ever since this happened, I've been wondering if I'm losing my marbles. I splashed some water on my face, and I think I'm ready to continue. What do you want to ask me?"

"Well, it's more about what you want to tell us. Do you think we've missed anything out? I have testimony from the security staff on duty that night that Mr Robson didn't leave the hospital, which agrees with your account; I will interview your colleagues but I'm expecting their explanations to be very similar to yours, as their written reports are."

"So where do we go from here?" Matron butted in. "I am confident that my nurses are telling the truth, and there isn't any evidence from other hospital staff to the contrary. Mr Robson is obviously wasting our time and causing my people unnecessary stress."

Tim shifted uneasily in his seat. "Well, I agree with what you've just said, but for the fact that this complaint is interspersed with a complaint against the duty doctor. Julia here and her colleagues have reported that Dr, er," he ran his finger down a document "Here it is. Dr Robert Greenway was not negligent, contrary to what Dr Jamila Kaur claimed. The implication from Dr Kaur's statement is that Staff is complicit in Dr Greenway's negligence." They sat in silence for a moment, looking at each other. "Let's call a halt here, shall we? Not that it's finished, but I might make more progress by interviewing the other nurses and the doctors before we resume. Agreed?" The others nodded gravely, and Tim left. Julia burst into tears and Matron took her hand.

"Don't let it get on top of you, Julia," she said. "I have no reason to disbelieve what you said. Come and have a cup of coffee and a cake in the staff canteen." They got up and left.

## Chapter 4

Tim and Bob sat on opposite sides of the table.

"Now then, Dr Greenway," Tim began hesitantly. "I'm sure you realise the gravity of the situation. If it weren't for the testimonies of the nurses you'd be in pretty hot water at the moment."

"Yes, I understand that, and please call me 'Bob', but I am telling the truth, and the patient was dead when I first examined him, and he was dead again on the next night and Dr Solomon confirmed it. I can't explain what happened next, but if he'd been dead and I said he was alive I imagine I'd be in equally hot water."

"Quite. Got to admit, Bob, I've never had a case like this before, and I've been handling complaints for twenty years. Can we go through the facts again? I know you've already done it several times, but just in case either of us has missed something."

"What is there to miss? But okay, if you want to hear it all again I'll tell you again."

They went through the entire tale again, and at the end Tim agreed it was exactly the same as the first time.

"Thanks, Bob. Now I'll interview Dr Solomon. I agree none of this makes sense, but I have procedures to follow. Dr Kaur might have to wait until tomorrow. I'm not looking forward to that. Not that she's dishonest or anything, but she's always right and anyone who disagrees with her is, by definition, wrong, if you know what I mean. But I didn't say that."

Tim's interviews with the other doctors and second interviews with the nursing staff only confirmed what he had already been told. Time to interview Mr Robson again.

"Look, I've already told you what happened, and I've told you again, and you still don't believe me. I want those nurses sacked. They turned a sick old man out into the cold in the middle of the night wearing next to nothing then they call me a liar and say it wasn't their fault. I need to take this to the papers. You asked me not to but I'm not getting any satisfaction and now you and your team are calling me a liar again.,"

"Let's be calm about this, Mr Robson."

"Calm? I've been calm and where has it got me? Nowhere. I want those nurses and that doctor off the premises so no other family can suffer the way we have."

The following night exactly the same thing happened. Mr Robson Snr was spotted by Lorraine trying to escape. This time she shouted and gave chase immediately, trying to follow him. Julia and Marian followed too, but once again, he went through the door at the end of the ward and disappeared. When he appeared at the foot of his grandson's bed, his son was ready for him. He grabbed the old man and held him while his wife wrapped a rug around his shoulders, and they put him in the car together. Mrs Robson slammed the car door but by the time Mr Robson had got to the other side and got in the car his father had vanished. There was a stretch of grass between their house and the road, and there in the middle of it was the old man and his grandson, holding hands and walking away. Mr and Mrs Robson gave chase, but no matter how fast they ran they couldn't catch the pair. When they reached the road they vanished, and Mr and Mrs

Robson stared at one another in disbelief. Then they realised their son, Tyler, was out there somewhere in flimsy pyjamas possibly with his granddad. Rushing back to the house they found him sat up in bed smiling. After some coaxing they got out of him that Granddad had been, but Tyler hadn't left the house. His feet were clean and dry, and he wasn't at all cold. This was a relief, but who did they see walking across the grass with Dad? Once Tyler was settled in bed they went downstairs and Mrs Robson telephoned the hospital demanding an explanation while Mr Robson telephoned the police and insisted they go to the hospital to arrest the staff on that ward for gross negligence. The police at first tried to explain that in such a case they wouldn't treat it as an emergency but would take steps the next day, but Mr Robson pointed out that the safety of the other patients was at risk, perhaps their lives too, and felt the papers would be interested in the local constabulary refusing to act in an emergency. Reluctantly they sent two officers to the hospital.

The security guard escorted the two police officers up to the ward and introduced them to Staff Nurse Julia. She stood there, arms folded, with a sceptical frown.

"I suppose you're here about Mr Robson?" she asked in a rather unfriendly tone of voice.

"That's right," one officer said, glancing at her colleague. They could tell by Julia's mannerisms that this wasn't going to be straight forward.

"Follow me," Julia instructed them and set off at a brisk pace into one of the rooms. She pointed at an elderly man asleep in bed. "This is Mr Robson. Look above the bed. It says 'Mr Raymond Robson, prefers to be called Ray'. Look here," she gently picked up his arm and showed them the name tag around his wrist. "It says here that he is Mr Raymond Robson. What else do you want to see? Have I convinced you that this is him? Is he here or is he not?"

"Well, slow down a bit," the officer said anxiously. "You're telling us this and you don't know why we're here yet."

"You're here because his son, Mr Angry, wants to make trouble for me. You should be arresting him for wasting police time and for accusing me and my staff of doing things we haven't done! Are you satisfied with what I've shown you?"

"Yes, but how did you know that's why we are here?"

"This is the third time in three days he has accused us of losing his father. Now you're welcome to carry out any further checks you need to make to be certain that we haven't 'lost' Mr Robson, but when you're finished I would like you to go. The doctor and I are being investigated for losing this poor man, and two of my best nurses are being taken away to somewhere they can do less damage. As you can see, we haven't lost him, but the authorities have to investigate what the idiot says."

The officers thanked Julia for her co-operation, apologised and left, scratching their heads. Julia went into the restroom, slamming the door behind her, and one of the nurses came in to make her a cup of coffee and give her a hug.

Despite the counter accusation of him losing his own father in his car in the middle of the night on two separate occasions, Mr Robson refused to be placated with anything other than the removal of the nurses and doctors involved in the case. After a great deal of work by the legal department Staff Nurse Julia and Dr Bob were moved to a different NHS hospital in the town. The intention was to move Marian and Lorraine there as soon as suitable vacancies arose. Then the HR department received a letter from a private hospital which had just opened. They offered temporary posts for the two nurses (how did they know about them?), fully funded, including pension contributions sick pay and holiday pay, until they were able to return to NHS posts. The head of HR was a bit suspicious, but her doubts were allayed when she visited the new hospital and discovered it was run very much along NHS lines, and the nurses would be well looked after until their return was possible. The paperwork was completed in a week and they were invited to start work there the following Monday, Lorraine at eight in the morning and Marian later the same day.

Lorraine was met at the door by a young man in a smart uniform and escorted to the lift.

"You're to work on Ward 27," the security officer told her. She got in and pressed the button for Ward 27. When she got out she was met by a nurse in a conventional uniform, but of a strange turquoise colour. The nurse introduced herself as the ward Sister, shook hands, and led Lorraine through a door to a short corridor with a door leading to the staff room.

"This the staff room where we eat and rest and change our clothing. Locker 7b has been allocated to you. Here is the key. In it you will find your uniform. Please change into it as quickly as possible." Sister handed her the key and left. Lorraine was impressed by the quality of the furnishings and kitchen equipment but felt the Sister had been a bit cold when it came to welcoming a new starter. Other than this there was nothing to complain about. She made herself a cup of coffee and changed while waiting for it to cool. The new uniform was of the same turquoise colour as she had already seen. It was of good quality material and fitted perfectly, and had her forename embroidered on it. Sister returned just as Lorraine was finishing her coffee.

"Put that down," she said, quietly but firmly. "Follow me." Lorraine did as instructed. At the nursing station they stopped to collect a wheeled stand bearing all the equipment Lorraine was used to. "Your task is to carry out obs on the patients in rooms one, two and three. Each room contains four patients. When you are finished you may take a ten minute break in the staff room for tea or coffee or other drink, and something to eat. Food and drink are not permitted anywhere except in the staff room. After your break you will start again in room one. At twelve o'clock you may have a thirty minute lunch break. Lunch is provided. You will find it in the cupboards and fridge in the staff room. Personal food may not be brought in for fear of introducing germs or other forms of contamination. Do you understand?"

Lorraine nodded. "Yes, Sister," she replied, thinking the rules were more strict than was necessary.

"Good," said Sister. "Begin. I'll be here for part of the morning to answer any questions."

Lorraine forced a smile. Sister was neither friendly nor hostile but was strangely distant. She took her trolley into room one and went to the first bed. The lady in it, who looked about eighty, appeared to be in a coma, but she pressed on. She started with the pulse. There wasn't one. She checked the patient's breathing. She wasn't breathing. She ran to the nursing station.

"Sister, this lady is dead!" she said urgently.

"No matter," said Sister without looking up from her work. "Continue with your duties. When you have finished with her go on to the next patient." Lorraine stood there looking flustered. "What are you waiting for? Please return to your duties. You do know how to do obs, don't you?"

"Yes, Sister," she nodded. "Of course I do, but I thought you would need to know the lady is dead."

"I already know. Please continue."

Lorraine returned to the patient, Mrs Anderson. She checked the pulse and breathing just to make sure, then tried to do the blood pressure and all the other routine tests. Mrs Anderson was definitely dead. She filled in the chart on the board at the foot of the bed and moved on to the next. This lady too was dead. She felt a bit apprehensive about disturbing Sister, who probably knew this one was dead too. And so on for the other ladies in the room. Rooms two and three also contained dead patients. That's all they contained. No empty beds; no living patients; dead bodies all perfectly dressed in official hospital nightwear. Lorraine shuddered as she left room three, wheeling the stand back to the nursing station. Sister didn't look up from her work so Lorraine didn't speak. Back in the staff room she wondered whether to make a coffee for Sister but decided against it. She made her own coffee and found a plastic box of biscuits in the cupboard. She helped herself to two, one chocolate and the other plain and sat down on the very comfortable chair in the corner of the room, ate her biscuit, and closed her eyes waiting for her coffee to cool. What was going on? Suddenly she was disturbed by noise out in the ward. She got up to investigate, but the staff room door wouldn't open. She felt trapped, as there was no other door. The window only opened at the very top and fully open was only about six inches wide. Lorraine was quite slim, but even she wouldn't be able to get through there and there was a drop of some seventy or eighty feet to the ground. She hammered on the door and shouted but no-one came.

## Chapter 5

Lorraine was wondering what to do when she heard a click from the door. Trying the handle showed it to be unlocked, but there was no-one anywhere nearby. Looking at her watch she realised her ten minutes was up, so she washed her hands, collected her stand, and proceeded to room one. She was reluctant to ask any questions as Sister seemed to know everything. At the first bed she immediately noticed that this was not Mrs Anderson. It was Mrs Richards. She too was dead. The other ladies in the room were also new, also dead, but she did the tests and updated the charts. On to room two and these ladies were all different, all dead, as were all the men in room three. At the end of this pass she returned to the staff room for her next break to find her former colleague, Marian, being given the rules by Sister. Sister turned to Lorraine.

"I understand you know one another," she said.

"Yes, we do," they chorused, smiling. Sister didn't smile but turned back to Marian and continued reciting the rules. After Sister left Marian changed into her new uniform. Lorraine had already gone back to the ward to start the next pass, finding yet more new but dead people in her three rooms. Unfortunately, their tea breaks didn't coincide, so they didn't have an opportunity until later in the day when Sister left.

"What's going on?" Marian asked in a whisper as soon as Sister had left. "I've got a load of dead people here but I'm doing obs. What's the point?"

"Mine are the same, and they get replaced every now and again when I'm having a break. I never see them being changed, but every now and then I get locked in the staff room and that's when it seems to be happening."

"Well, I don't want to complain because we've escaped from the investigation, not that we did anything wrong, but you know what it can be like when the press get their hands on things, but I'm not sure about this place."

"Me neither," answered Lorraine. "Sister isn't like a real person. She never smiles, never gives away any emotion, never has a conversation about anything other than work, almost like she isn't human."

"I'm not happy about this," said Marian after a brief time in thought. "I'm going to ask to be told why we're doing this. What's the point of doing obs on dead bodies?"

A couple of hours later Sister came in and went straight to her desk at the nursing station and began her work. She didn't speak to either nurse, didn't even acknowledge their existence when they greeted her. When Marian had finished her routine on her side of the ward she didn't go to the rest room for her coffee break. She went to the nursing station and confronted Sister.

"We would like to know why we're doing this. What is the point of doing obs on dead bodies? And why are they changed every few hours for a different set of dead bodies? It doesn't make sense and I think there's something fishy about all this. I want an explanation and I want it now." She stood at the entrance of the nursing station so that Sister couldn't get out, widened her stance and fold her arms firmly across her chest, in the style of a night-club bouncer. Sister seemed entirely unperturbed. She looked up and smiled a sweet but rather false smile.

"You don't know?" she asked. "Do you really not understand?"

"If I knew would I be standing here like this?"

"Well, no. Let's not be confrontational. I'll tell you why. Let's have a cup of tea over it." She got up and followed Marian to the rest room. Lorraine followed too and made tea for them all. When they were seated around the table with their cups Sister smiled again.

"You have the gift. That's why you're here. Didn't you know that?"

The two nurses glanced at one another and shook their heads. "No, we didn't know we had a gift," said Lorraine. "What is it?"

"Why were you taken out of the other hospital?"

"Because Mr Robson's son wanted to make trouble," Marian answered. Sister shook her head.

"No. Tell me what happened and put it in the simplest terms possible. Forget about the trouble-making son."

"Well, Lorraine here was doing the obs, and she heard Mr Robson get out of bed and head for the exit. She called to him, but he left the ward. We chased after him, but he escaped. Next time she looked in his room he was dead, so she called Staff, who examined him and called the doctor. Then the next day another doctor examined him, and he wasn't dead. We don't understand this, none of us. Then it all happened again, twice more, then they took us off that ward. Then they sent us here. Didn't give us a choice; we got the impression that if we didn't come here we might lose our jobs. Lorraine is a young lass, but I'd struggle to get any other work at my age, so we came here. Please explain this – we don't understand."

"Let me put it into simpler terms for you. You examined a dead person and he came back to life. Not immediately, but later. That's what you do here. You examine dead people then we take them away and hopefully they will come back to life. This is your gift. People will pay money for this. Try telling me it isn't a gift if you want, but I won't believe you. But for now, I need to get back to my work, and so do you." She got up and went back to the nursing station. They gave her time to get out of earshot then leant forward across the table.

"I don't like this," Marian whispered. "I'm going to investigate when I get home tonight." They were just about to go back to work when they heard the rest room door click. They tried the handle, but they were locked in. Fifteen minutes later it clicked again, and they were released. Their patients were all gone and replaced by a new cohort.

That evening after Sister had left Marian went to the lift. She called it and it came, but when she got in there was only one button. Ward 27. That being the only option she pressed it and the door closed then opened again immediately. She called to Lorraine and they tried it again, but ended up back where they started. The went to the other end of the ward and went through the doors only to be faced with a blank wall. Back in the lift there was still only one button. They returned to the rest room.

"What are we going to do?" Lorraine asked in a bit of a panic. "We're stuck here!" She was getting quite worked up over this, so Marian gave her a hug.

"I've been thinking," she said. "What time does it feel like?"

"Middle of the day," Lorraine replied, drying her eyes and looking at Marian in amazement. "Why do you ask?"

"It can't be," Marian said. "How many times have we done rounds of obs? About twenty. And how long does each one take? About twenty minutes. And how many tea breaks and lunch breaks have we had? About four tea breaks and one lunch break. We have been here for more than seven hours. What time is it?"

Lorraine looked at her watch. "Half past one," she replied slowly. She glanced up at the clock on the wall. "It's half past one, but it can't be."

"And what have we had to eat and drink? The stuff they provided. I mean, it's nice, it's good quality stuff, but perhaps it's drugging us!"

"You mean because we just eat their stuff we don't know what's happening to us?"

"Exactly. If we hadn't stopped to think we might have been just going on and on for ever, just doing obs all day every day, never going home, never seeing our families again."

The door opened and Sister came in. "What are you doing sitting here? You're supposed to be out there doing obs."

"No, we want to be out. We know what you're up to."

"If you don't do your rounds of obs you won't get any food or drink and you won't be let out if you do or you don't. You belong to the company. You have the gift, and your only option is to use it. Do I make myself clear?"

Marian lurched at her, but she got away and slammed the door shut before Marian could reach the much younger woman. When they went out back into the ward Sister had disappeared. Marian and Lorraine looked at one another in disbelief. Lorraine burst into tears. Marian hugged her for a moment.

"Come on, girl, looks like we're stuck here. I'm pleased you're a nice lass, 'cos it looks like we're going to be together for a long time. Let's get back to work."

# The Winter Wedding

## Chapter 1

Dan wandered into the kitchen looking rather vague but cross at the same time. "Not looking forward to this," he said grumpily.

"Come on, you'll enjoy it when we get there. Cassandra and Algernon have been dear friends for more than twenty years and I haven't seen them for ages. And weddings can be fun once you've had a small glass of shandy or two to loosen up," Maisie replied looking up from the instructions she was writing for Stephanie.

"Yes, I know," Dan replied. "I'm looking forward to seeing them again. It's not them I'm cross about. It's having to spend too much time with Maureen and Horace."

"Don't be rude about Maureen. She's my sister, my only sister, and she means a lot to me, despite being a bit dizzy, so don't go complaining about her!"

"No. She's alright, in her own way. It's her moron of a husband. It's okay for you. You and Maureen go off into a corner and giggle like silly schoolgirls for hours at a time, leaving me to entertain him. He's unbelievably boring, and his politics aren't to my liking. Reads the Daily Telegraph and thinks it might give a balanced view if it weren't so far to the left. What are you doing?"

"Instructions for Stephanie. I've put seven meals in the freezer – all she has to do is defrost them and cook them and try not to poison the little ones."

"Don't be silly. She can cook better than I can. Don't forget when she's away at uni. she cooks for herself, and from what I hear, she cooks for her flat mates too. She's sensible and organised. They'll be fine."

"Yes, I know, but I still worry. It's a mother's job to worry. But yes, you're right. So have you packed your toiletries? You know, shaving kit and other such mysteries."

"Sorry, dear, I thought you'd done that."

"No. I packed all the clothes, yours and mine, and other things and the presents, but I don't do shaving stuff. That way you can't blame me for getting it wrong."

"Oh. I only came in here for a coffee, but there isn't any. Shall I make a pot?"

"Yes but pack your stuff while it's percolating." Stephanie came in, smiling. "Stephanie, darling, I was just about to call you."

"Oh dear. I heard the word 'coffee' and thought it represented an opportunity," she announced and threw herself into a chair."

"Don't worry, dear. I'm just writing instructions for you so that everyone has a balanced diet while we're away."

"Oh, Mum! I don't believe this! I know more about balanced diets than you ever will."

"I tried to tell her that, but you know what she's like," Dan muttered under his breath. Stephanie gave him a wink.

"Okay then, what do I have to do?"

Maisie went through the notes while Stephanie pretended to listen, nodding at appropriate places. Dan was making the coffee when he looked out of the kitchen window to see a big luxury car pull up on their drive.

"They're here," he announced with total lack of enthusiasm. "Noreen! Nicholas! Your cousins are arriving. Go and help them get their stuff in!" he called through the kitchen door. He got mugs from the cupboard and milk from the fridge. "I suppose they'll want coffee before we set off."

Maisie ran to the door and flung it open, greeting her twin sister with hugs and kisses and they both started talking at the same time, then dissolved into manic laughter. "Do come in. Dan's just made a fresh pot of coffee." She leant forward to give Horace a peck on the cheek then fussed over Jemima and Joshua. "Gosh! Haven't you grown!"

"That's what children do, dear," Dan pointed out. "I don't think they much different to our pair." Maisie summoned her children and made all four stand in line, only to discover that they were all more or less the same height. "Help Jemima and Joshua get their stuff up to your rooms then come back down for some coffee. They've had quite a journey and will want to rest a bit."

"No, Uncle Dan," Joshua spoke up. "It wasn't tiring. We rested in the car. It's a big car, you know, and good for resting in." The other children laughed and carried the bags upstairs. Dan greeted Maureen with a kiss and shook Horace's hand gravely.

"How's it going, old bean?" said Horace, then turned away without waiting for a reply. They all sat down with coffee. "Damn nuisance, this wedding thing. A long way to drive at this time of year. We'd planned to spend Christmas in Thailand but had to cancel."

"We can drive if you want," said Dan with a grin.

"Good heavens! No! I'd never hear the last of it if Maureen got some cow poo off your Land Rover on her million pound dress."

"I'm sure it wasn't a million pounds."

"No, but the way she goes on about it you'd think it was." They all laughed at this except Maureen who felt uncomfortable. "No, I don't mind driving, as long as the weather holds."

"Well I think it's very good of them to have the wedding during the holidays and to put us up in their castle, or whatever it is" Maisie commented. "My work's very quiet until the end of January when they all realise they need to submit tax returns, and Dan's got Eddie to look after emergencies until we get back. Surely your business is quiet over Christmas?"

Horace nodded, "Yes, but I wanted a proper holiday instead of sitting around drinking for a week."

"But if we were in Thailand you'd just be sitting around drinking for a week!" offered Maureen. They all laughed again. Stephanie came in and poured herself a coffee. "Stephanie, darling, it's wonderful of you to look after our brats as well as your own siblings," Maureen gushed, stroking Stephanie's long hair. "I do like your hair, sweetie."

"Thank, Aunty Maureen. I've got some theories to try out on them. Stuff I learned at uni. Thought control and stuff." She grinned and left the room, coffee in hand.

"Well, I hope it's all legal," said Maureen. She paused in her drink when she realised the others were all staring at her.

"Of course it will be legal," said Dan breaking the silence. "She's *our* daughter, not yours." The silence returned.

## Chapter 2

The parents all bundled into Horace's big car while Stephanie rounded up the children. "Come along," she chivvied, a bit like a mother hen. "Your olds want to see happy smiling faces waving good-bye. Don't worry, you can have fun once they're out of the way." Jemima and Joshua weren't sure what to make of this, but Noreen and Nicholas seemed quite relaxed, so they decided to play along and see what was what.

"Oh, by the way, here are the keys to the Land Rover, darling," said Dan as he handed Stephanie a bunch of keys through the car window. "Shouldn't need it, but just as well to have them, just in case, and remember to let it warm up before you start it if the weather turns frosty."

"Thanks, Dad. I know how to drive it – done it before when you and Mum had too much to drink last Christmas. Remember?"

The big car drove slowly away, picking up speed when it reached the road, and was soon out of sight. Stephanie chivvied them inside, as it was starting to snow. "Right. Up to your rooms and unpack what you need to unpack then back down here for squash and biscuits. Go!" Five minutes later they were back and sat in the living room around the coffee table where Stephanie had deposited a tray of beakers, a jug of blackcurrant squash and three plates of assorted biscuits. "Right. This is what the score is. I don't want you under my feet all the time, and I'm sure you don't want me towering over you bossing you about all the time either, so for breakfast we all help ourselves to cereal and toast, then we put the stuff in the dishwasher, then I make lunch, perhaps with some help, and that will be the main meal of the day. When the stuff is back in the dishwasher your time is your own. At tea-time we have a light snack, then you're free of me for the rest of the day. I have some things I need to do up in my room, so don't bother me and I won't bother you. If there's an emergency or something you're not happy about, come up and knock on my door. I'll always be available no matter what time of day or night, but don't be surprised at what you might see. Or shocked or frightened. Anything in my room is harmless as long as you don't touch it. Noreen and Nick, you are the hosts, so I expect you to help Josh and Jemima with where things are for breakfast and everything else. And no fighting or other naughtiness, or there will be unreasonable punishments. Understand?"

"Yes, we understand," they chorused.

"Good. We're all on holiday so let's have fun. Within reason, of course. I'm about to prepare lunch. Anyone want to help?" Jemima and Noreen volunteered, and the boys started a game of chess. "The girls are helping today, so I expect the boys to help tomorrow. No gender-based rolls in this house," she called over her shoulder.

"She always was different," Joshua whispered, "but she seems more different."

"Yes," Nicholas replied. "She's been strange ever since she came back from uni. Spends hours in her room. Sometimes we only see her at meal times. But nothing to worry about. I think."

Lunch was lasagne with garlic bread, followed by tiramisu, which they all enjoyed. Once the dishwasher was loaded up Stephanie disappeared up to her room. Nicholas and Joshua returned to their game of chess while Noreen and Jemima sat on the rug in front of the fire and looked at magazines for a while. When the boys had finished their game Joshua went to the window to have a look out. "There's a lot of snow out there," he announced. "I'm glad we're in here with a good fire." He and Nicholas sat down by the fire with the girls. "I was saying to Nick earlier," he said in a lowered voice, just in case Stephanie could hear, "Steph seems a bit different to what she used to be."

"Yes, I thought that too," said Jemima, "but I didn't want to mention it."

"This is only her first term at uni.," replied Noreen, "but she's come home with some strange ideas."

"Such as?" asked Joshua.

"Well, that's just it," said Nicholas. "Nothing you can put your finger on. Obviously her politics are a bit further to the left than they used to be, but other things, such as when we're watching the news and Mum criticises someone for having strange hair or clothes not only does she defend the person, which is fair enough, but she goes on to accuse Mum of dressing strangely when she was that age, totally without proof because in all the pictures of Mum as a young person she was dressed in what to me look like boring gear. Fashion wasn't Mum's strong point. Good job she doesn't live with you. Aunt Maureen was quite the fashion lady and Uncle Horace is a bit to the right of Thatcher. There'd be rows every day."

"Yes," added Noreen, "but that's just the obvious part. She's strange in a strange sort of way. Like Nick says, nothing you can put your finger on. It's as though she's up to something and doesn't want the rest of the world to know about it."

They sat chatting until they heard Stephanie's footsteps coming down the stairs. "Tea-time!" she announced. "I thought crumpets would do as we had quite a large meal for lunch. You can have whatever you want on them – jam, honey, Marmite, peanut butter, anything else you fancy?" They shook their heads, but she didn't see as she was already in the kitchen. They followed her.

"No, thanks, they will be fine," Jemima replied, having pulled a face at the thought of Marmite on crumpets.

"Good. Let's get started. Lend a hand. Someone put the kettle on and milk the cups. Get some plates and cutlery out. Get a wriggle on or it will be bedtime." Stephanie put about ten crumpets on the big grill pan and pushed it into the grill. Joshua and Jemima weren't used to a big farmhouse-style kitchen and watched open mouthed while Nicholas and Noreen saw to the crockery and cutlery very efficiently, knowing where everything was. Nothing like that in her house. After the crumpets Stephanie produced a fruit cake Maisie had made the day before, and they ate that with cheese.

"I say, Steph," Joshua muttered through a mouthful of crumbs, "Aunty Maisie certainly know how to do a good cake. Our mum is useless at stuff like this." The others tried not to laugh. After the meal they loaded up the dishwasher and set it away and Stephanie disappeared upstairs. They sat on the sofas with beakers of squash.

"What's on TV?" Nicholas asked.

"Nothing," replied Noreen. "When the weather's like this we don't get a decent enough signal out here. We're miles from the nearest town and some of the hills block the signal."

"I've got an idea," said Joshua. "I brought something along just in case we ran out of things to do. I'll go and get it." He disappeared upstairs.

"Oh no!" sighed Jemima. "Not that stupid thing!"

Nicholas and Noreen were about to ask when Joshua came in carrying a cardboard box which he placed on the floor by the coffee table. He unloaded a game board which he placed in the middle of the table, and a small glass which would have been a whisky tumbler if it had been taller. The board had the letters of the alphabet and the digits nought to nine arranged in a circle, and 'yes' and 'no' in the middle. "It called 'Ouija!' and its fun," he announced. Nicholas and Noreen glanced at each other as Jemima covered her eyes. "We all put a finger on the glass, and it answers our questions. Honest. It's fun!"

"Well, I'm not sure this is a good idea," said Nicholas. "Jemima obviously doesn't like it."

"Take no notice of her," Joshua replied with a sneer. "She just doesn't like it because it's my game and it has a bit of edge, unlike her feeble games. Come on. Give it a go."

Nicholas and Noreen glanced at each other. Joshua explained what to do and Nicholas nodded to Noreen and they each put a finger on the glass, which was upturned in the middle of the board. Jemima sat back in the armchair, arms folded and scowling.

"I'll go first, to show you how harmless it is," he said. "What is Jemima's favourite colour?" The glass moved slowly, spelling out the word 'purple'.

"Is that true?" Noreen asked her. Jemima nodded. "Okay, but he probably knew that. Ask something you couldn't possibly know."

"What is Uncle Dan's favourite food?" It spelled out 'curry'. Nick and Noreen looked at each other in amazement. "What kind of curry?" Joshua asked, confident he had made progress with them. The glass spelled out 'lamb vindaloo'. Nicholas and Noreen were astounded.

"Okay," said Nicholas slowly. "I'll ask it a question I couldn't possibly know. What colour nightdress was Jemima wearing last night?" The glass spelled out 'pink'. "Is that true, Jemima?" She nodded her head, looking a bit nervous. They asked it seven or eight more questions, mainly harmless, and it answered every one correctly. Joshua grinned in triumph. "Seems harmless enough, so far," commented Nicholas. "Come on, Jemima, put your finger on the glass too, and we can each take turns as being off the glass when it's something we might know."

Reluctantly Jemima moved from the armchair to one of the little stools the others were on around the coffee table. "Let's ramp up the tension a bit," said Joshua. "What is Steph's bra size?" No sooner were the words out of his mouth when there was a bang, and he was flung off his stool to the side. When he got up, they noticed a handprint on the side of his face, as though he had been slapped really hard. He got back onto the stool, rubbing his face.

"Perhaps we should put this away for now," said Noreen.

"We don't want anyone else to get hurt." Nicholas agreed, and put it back into the box, despite Joshua's protests. "It's nearly bedtime. Does anyone want a hot drink?" They all agreed on hot chocolate so Noreen went into the kitchen to make it. Jemima went to lend a hand.

"What happened there?" Nicholas asked in a whisper when the girls were out of the room.

"Don't really know," Joshua replied. "It's never happened before. Feels like I've been slapped. Really hard."

"Is this why Jemima didn't want to do it?"

"No. Like I said, this is the first time. She's scared it will reveal what colour her knickers are, or what she got up to with the boys at school. Shh! They're coming back."

They sat chatting while they drank the hot chocolate and munched on some biscuits. The door opened and Stephanie came in.

"Well, thanks for making me a drink, guys!"

"Sorry, Steph," said Noreen. "I thought about it, but you'd said you didn't want to be disturbed."

"Okay, I'll let you off this time. Josh! What's happened to your face?"

"Dunno. It just happened while we were doing the game."

"Happened? Did someone do this to you?"

"No. Like I said. It just happened." The others nodded in agreement.

"Come into the kitchen. I'll tend to it while someone makes me a drink." He followed her, and Noreen followed too, and set about boiling the kettle again. Stephanie sat Joshua on a stool beside the kitchen sink. She ran her hand under the cold tap for a while, then she put it on the handprint, holding his head still with the other. Her hand fitted the handprint perfectly. Noreen saw this but tried not to make a sound.

"I'll put your drink on the coffee table," Noreen said, in an attempt to hide her gasp. She took the drink through to the other room.

"Just stay there, I'll put some soothing cream on it," she said to Joshua, drying his face gently with a towel. Returning from the cupboard with a blue and white tube she gently rubbed the cream in. "34B by the way, but it's none of your business," she whispered. They went through and sat with the others, chatting and finishing their drinks. "Okay, bedtime!" Stephanie declared. Jemima cleared the mugs and biscuits into the kitchen and they trooped up the stairs to the bedrooms.

## Chapter 3

The boys were asleep in no time, but the girls lay chatting for a while.

"I don't have anything against the game," said Jemima. "It's more about what he does with it. He seems to go out of his way to embarrass me. I know we're all family and we've known each other all our lives, but when his pals are in, he delights in telling them about my undies or any of my clothes that don't fit or anything embarrassing or stupid I've done."

"Boys are like that. I know Nick isn't. He used to be, but Dad had a talk with him about it when I, you know, became a woman, and he hasn't done it since."

"My Daddy is useless at stuff like that. So is Mummy, actually. Your parents are so much better than mine."

"Well, yes, I suppose they are. I'm lucky. And they had Steph to practice on."

They both giggled at that, and eventually dropped off to sleep.

Stephanie sat on the floor in her room in the lotus position and surrounded by tea lights. Her eyes were closed and her breathing was very slow. She was concentrating on what Mum and Dad were doing. They were too far away for her to see clearly, but she could tell that mum was happy and slightly drunk. Dad was a bit grumpy, having had to listen to Uncle Horace for some hours. She tried to tune in on Uncle Horace and Aunty Maisie, but she couldn't. Never mind. She planted a thought in Mum's head that the children were okay, put out the candles, and went to bed. Her sleep was disturbed. How had Joshua got through to her so easily? Did he know he'd done that? Need to keep an eye on him over the next few days. Thank goodness they're only staying until the weekend. She wondered if Mum had got the message. Her parents didn't know she had this ability. It was somethjng she learned at university from a friend whose mother was a witch. That's what the friend said. What qualifies you as a witch? Had she become a witch by learning to do this? Witch or not, she could do it. She would try it out on Joshua if he played up too much. Why did he want to know her bra size? Nick never asked. Or did Nick already know from inspecting the washing basket? The next morning, she woke up feeling very unrefreshed. Sorting out breakfast for the children took her mind off it, and she caught forty winks while the younger children filled up the dishwasher. Lunchtime came and went – lamb casserole, which was easy to heat up, and which was enjoyed by everyone. When the plates were all in the dishwasher Stephanie went up to her room and the others went into the living room. Noreen got the Monopoly out of the cupboard before anyone else had a chance to speak, and they played until teatime. Stephanie came down and announced that they were having cheese on toast, followed by a fruit cake she herself had made. They all agreed that even though Maisie's cake had been excellent, this was even better.

This cake is the best cake I've ever tasted! Even better than Aunty Maisie's! And having it with a slice of cheese is pure genius!" declared Joshua, to which the other three all nodded their agreement.

"Why, thank-you, Josh. That's very kind of you to say that." She smiled mischievously. "Didn't Aunty Maureen do cookery at school?" They shrugged their shoulders.

"From what I've overheard," said Nicholas, "she didn't do much at school."

"Now Nick, that's unkind," Stephanie scolded. "Even if it might be true." They all burst out laughing, spraying cake crumbs everywhere.

After tea Joshua got the Ouija board out again. "Oh, no! Not that thing again!" exclaimed Jemima. "I thought you would've had enough after getting hurt yesterday. I can still see the mark on your face. What will Mum say if it's still there when they get back?"

"Look, we'll give it a go and at the first sign of anything going wrong it'll go back in the box. Okay?" Joshua replied.

"You're not the only one here. What about Noreen and Nick? Don't they get a say? It is their house after all."

"I'm cool with it," said Nicholas. "But we must stick rigidly to that condition – if anything starts to go wrong it goes back in the box straight away. You okay with that, Noreen?"

"Yes, totally. If things even look like they might be going wrong it goes back in the box."

That settled, they sat on the stools around the table, fingers on the glass. Noreen decided to set a sensible example. "What will I be when I grow up?" The glass moved very slowly to spell out the word 'vet'. "Good. That's what I want to be."

"My turn next," announced Nicholas. "What will I be when I grow up?" Again, the glass moved slowly, this time to spell out 'teacher'. "Well, that's a surprise! I hadn't given that any thought, but it's worth considering. Your turn, Jemima."

"What will I be when I grow up?" she asked, taking her finger off so she couldn't be accused of pushing it. It spelled out 'clerk'. She looked shocked. "Clerk? What's one of them? Never heard of that job before!"

Nicholas and Noreen glanced at one another. "It's an admin job," Noreen explained. "Doing paperwork in offices. Don't you know what a clerk is?"

"No," Jemima replied grumpily. "I don't know much. We're not like you. And it sounds a bit boring, doing paperwork all day. I wish I had your parents."

"Don't say things like that," scolded Joshua. "Look at all the stuff they give us! We have a big house, big cars, loads of toys and games, posh clothes, money, things other kids don't have."

"Yes, but we know nothing. Did you know what a clerk was? And Nick and Noreen are properly cared for and loved. We just get money."

"Okay, let's change the subject," butted in Nicholas. "Your turn, Josh, but ask a different question."

"Okay. I'm going to ask it something difficult. We won't know if it's right or wrong. Not immediately, but it might give us something to laugh about. How old will my dad be when he dies?"

"That's a horrible question, Josh," exclaimed Noreen. "You don't deserve an answer." They all took their fingers off the glass, except Joshua. The glass moved, but not to the numbers. It spelled out 'already dead'. They looked at Joshua in silence. He took his finger off the glass.

"Shit. It's never been wrong before, but this, well it doesn't make sense."

"Let me try," said Nicholas. "How old will my dad be when he dies?" The glass moved to the eight, then the three. "Eighty-three. That sounds sensible. You do it, Noreen."

"How old will my dad be when he dies?" she asked, placing her finger on the glass. It went to the eight then the three. "Jemima? Are you going to try?"

"I suppose I'll have to, or I'll never hear the last of it." She placed her finger on the glass and asked the question. It spelled out 'already dead'. She got up and made for the door. Noreen tried to stop her, but she was pushed away roughly. Nicholas held Noreen back.

"Give her some time," he said. "Talk to her later."

Chapter 4

Jemima went upstairs and timidly knocked on Stephanie's door.

"Come in, Jemima," said Stephanie. Jemima gently turned the handle and slowly pushed the door open. She took two steps into the room and froze. She wasn't a very worldly person, especially when it came to exotic mystical practices, but this was totally beyond her comprehension. Stephanie was sitting on the floor in the lotus position wearing an extremely thin figure-hugging white nightdress. She was surrounded by tea lights and there were candles on every flat surface burning in different colours and giving off strange aromas. Jemima didn't know what to do. "Close the door, please, and do it gently so as not to disturb the candles." Jemima slowly pushed the door shut and just stood there. "Come in; have a seat. The floor's clean. Your monster brother has upset you. I understand." Stephanie untangled her legs and slid across the floor. She gave Jemima a hug. She held her until she felt the little girl relax. "That's better. He really can be a monster at times. Tell me what's bothering you the most. The fact that your father is already dead, or that your brother thought it an appropriate question to ask."

"How can Daddy be already dead? He was here just the other day!"

"Dear Jemima, there are many mysteries in the universe. Some don't make sense." Stephanie held her more tightly and wiped her tears. After a silence which seemed to last forever, but in actual fact was only a minute, she spoke again. "Remember I am always here for you, even when I am far away. Let's go downstairs and put your mind at rest." Stephanie rose to her feet and held Jemima's hands until she was up. She gave her another hug and a kiss and held her hand while they went into the living room. As they went in the room fell silent. Joshua was so embarrassed by the 'news' that he didn't notice Stephanie's sparce attire; Noreen and Nicholas were used to it and didn't bat an eyelid. They had obviously been discussing Jemima. Stephanie ushered her to the sofa next to Noreen then sat on the other side of her, holding her hand. She pointed at Joshua.

"You are a monster," she snarled at him. "You don't deserve to have these good people around you." She gesticulated at the others smiling. Her scowl returned as her gaze rested on Joshua again. "You deserve to be punished." She pointed at him, and he fell off his stool. The others remained silent. No-one got up to help him. They all stared at Stephanie. "Let's put this troublesome question to bed. Noreen, repeat the question Jemima asked."

"How old will Jemima's dad be when he dies?" she said, her lips trembling. 'Already dead' came the reply.

"Ask it again, this time from your point of view."

Noreen looked puzzled for a moment, then it suddenly dawned on her. "How old will Uncle Horace be when he dies?" The glass moved to the seven then to the three. They all stared at each other in silnce.

"Seventy-three!" exclaimed Nicholas. "I get it now. Uncle Horace isn't Jemima's dad!" Stephanie smiled, got up, and returned to her room. Jemima burst into tears and Noreen put her arm round her to comfort her. Joshua stared into space.

"That solves that mystery, but it gives us a new one," said Noreen, wiping Jemima's tears. "You do it, Nick, just to make sure."

Nick repeated both questions, getting the same answers Noreen had. "So Uncle Horace isn't your dad. Someone else is. I mean, he sort of is your dad, because he has been as long as you can remember, but he isn't your biological dad."

"How can Daddy not be my Daddy?" Jemima said slowly, obviously not understanding any of this. Joshua sat in silence.

Noreen and Nicholas glanced at each other. "We'll talk about this after we've gone to bed," said Noreen to Jemima quietly. "But for now, I think we should do something else." Nicholas agreed and put the Ouija stuff back into its box before Joshua had an opportunity to object. He glanced up at the clock.

"I think it might be time for hot chocolate, don't you think, Noreen?" Nicholas suggested. Noreen smiled and nodded.

"Good idea.," she said. "Go and put the kettle on. I'll be in in a minute to help." She dried Jemima's tears and started to get up, but Jemima grasped her arm.

"No, I'll go and help him," she mumbled and hurried off to the kitchen. Noreen and Joshua sat in an uncomfortable silence until the other two returned a few minutes later with a tray of drinks and biscuits. Jemima unloaded the drinks and biscuit plate onto the coffee table, then took a cup and a couple of biscuits up to Stephanie on the tray. Carefully she balanced the tray with one hand and was about to knock with the other when the door opened.

"Come in, Jemima," said Stephanie with a smile. Stephanie was seated on the floor, in the lotus position, as before.

"Er, how did you know it was me?" she asked hesitantly. She hadn't noticed earlier that Stephanie knew things she couldn't possibly know, but on this occasion Jemima was in more of a thinking mode – something that didn't happen very often.

"You are a decent girl and you wanted to thank me," Stephanie replied with a smile.

"But you knew it was me before, too."

"Oh, don't worry. I know lots of things, things I didn't know when I was your age. Do you want to have a chat?"

"I don't know. Perhaps tomorrow. I might have a chat with Noreen tonight. Someone my own age." She turned to go, then stopped by the door. "How much do you know about Daddy not being …" her voice trailed off.

"Not much. Nothing really, but I'll try to find out. You need to go downstairs. People of your own age."

"But how will you do that?"

"Never mind. Ways and means. Go. Remember I'm here for you. I love you; we all do. You're sweet – not like your brother." She smiled and gave her a wink. Jemima smiled back and returned to the living room.

The others had obviously been discussing the situation and fell silent as she came in. Noreen gesticulated to Jemima to sit next to her on the sofa. Joshua was in the armchair and Nicholas on the floor. They all sipped their chocolate, and each took a biscuit.

"Before you ask, Jemima," Nicholas began, "We know nothing about any of this. We're as much in the dark as you."

"Not quite as much, I fear," said Noreen. "Have you had the 'birds and bees' talk with your Mum, or at school?" she whispered to Jemima.

"Don't know what you're talking about. 'Birds and bees'?" she shook her head. Joshua began to laugh so Nicholas punched his leg which was quite close.

"Ow! What was that for?" Joshua complained.

"If you don't know, you're a bigger idiot than I thought," Nicholas answered with a scowl.

"Don't worry, Jemima," said Noreen putting her arm around Jemima's shoulders. "We'll have a girly chat tonight when we've gone to bed."

"I don't want to do anything else tonight," said Nicholas. "I'm going to do a crossword or read or something for half an hour then I'm off to bed."

"Good idea," said Noreen. "I suggest we all do the same."

Up in Noreen's bedroom the two girls got ready for bed. They sat cross legged on the floor, looking at each other. Noreen's face was full of trepidation, wondering where to start; Jemima looked as though it was a normal day, and they were about to discuss something trivial.

"Come on, then," Jemima began. "Birds and bees. I like nature."

"I assume your periods have started?" Noreen asked slowly.

"Yes, but what's that got to do with anything?"

"Did you ask your mum about that?" Jemima nodded. "And what did she say?"

"She said it's something that happens to women, and not to worry about it."

"Did she say why they happen?" Jemima shook her head, looking quite innocent.

"No. It's just something that happens to women."

Noreen rolled her eyes. "This is something that Aunty Maureen should have explained years ago, but she hasn't, and I don't think she will. Let's start with the birds and the bees. Actually, no, let's not. Didn't you have a talk about babies at school?"

"I think we did, but I missed it. I think that's when I was off with a broken arm."

"I see." Noreen cleared her throat and explained sex and the reproductive system in great detail. Two hours later Jemima's expression had changed to one of disbelief.

"How could Mummy be so stupid? I need to know this stuff." She flung her arms around Noreen and hugged her tightly. "Thank-you, Noreen. You might have saved me from something unspeakable." They hugged again as tears ran down Jemima's face.

"You explained that very well," said Stephanie. The other girls jumped because they hadn't heard her come in. "Very well indeed." Stephanie joined in the hug. "If you have any questions, come to Noreen, or me. Don't waste your time going to Aunty Maureen. She's useless. Think of us as your sisters, rather than cousins. We'll be here for you." When the hug ended Jemima burst into tears and the other two comforted her and dried her eyes. "Now do you understand how Daddy isn't Daddy?" Stephanie asked. Jemima nodded and dried her face again.

"Thank-you both. I think that's enough surprises for one night. Can we go to bed now?" Stephanie and Noreen smiled and nodded.

In Nicholas' room Joshua had got the Ouija board out of its box and placed it on the floor. Nicholas held Joshua's arm to stop him doing anything and they looked at each other sternly.

"Don't you think that thing's done enough damage for one night?" he said.

"You don't understand, Nick," Joshua replied with a pleading look in his eyes. "You know who your dad is. I don't. I need to know. And I'm going to have to explain this to Jemima. You saw what she was like – doesn't understand much and knows even less. I need to know so I can work out what to tell her and how to do it." Nicholas released his grip on Joshua's arm.

"Okay, I understand that. But on one condition – you tell me what you're going to ask before you ask it. Tell me your question before you touch the glass." Joshua nodded his agreement, and they placed the board in the middle of the floor and sat one on each side of it.

"Let's check what we already know first, just in case something has changed," suggested Nicholas.

"I don't see how it can, but yes, I see your point. You mean in case it wasn't being truthful." Nicholas nodded and they repeated the questions and got the same answers. "Okay. I want to ask my Dad's name." Nicholas nodded. They put their fingers on the glass and Joshua asked the question. The glass moved slowly to spell out 'Alf'. The boys looked at each other. "Who's Alf?" they asked simultaneously.

"I'm surprised you are messing about with that thing after all the grief it has caused this evening," said Stephanie in a stern voice. The boys jumped. Stephanie stood, hands on hips, by the door looking down on them with a scowl.

"Holy shit, Steph," exclaimed Nicholas. "I didn't hear you come in!" She picked up the board and the glass and put them back in the box.

"Look, Steph," said Joshua, trying to wrestle the box from her. "I don't know who my Dad is, and I need to know. What would you do if you didn't know yours?" She relaxed her grip on the box.

"Fair enough but be careful. You don't know what you might discover."

"We are being careful, Steph," interjected Nicholas. "He's telling me his question before he asks it, and I'll stop him if I think it isn't good. We know who our Dad is; he doesn't. He has a right to know." She nodded. They got the board and glass out again, and when they looked up Stephanie had disappeared.

"Wow! Where did she go to?" asked Joshua.

"Don't know. She just disappeared. I didn't hear her come in or go out, and it isn't possible to open that door without it creaking. Spooky."

"I was watching her all the time. Couldn't take my eyes of her when she wears things like that. She was almost not wearing anything, and I could see just about everything. Didn't you notice?"

"Well, no. We've grown up with her and don't notice stuff like that. But I did notice that she didn't come in or go out, and she seems to know what we're doing even when she isn't in the room. About time I had a chat with Noreen – see what she thinks."

"Pointless me having a chat with Jemima. She's clueless."

"She's got enough to worry about at the moment. Don't bother her. If Noreen and I come to a conclusion, we'll let you in on it. Anyway, I don't feel like doing any more of this tonight."

"But what about Alf? I need to know who my dad is!"

"Okay, but just another half hour at the most."

Joshua set up the board again, and asked who Alf is. 'Alf is dead' came the reply. Joshua wasn't pleased at this.

"No, look," said Nicholas. "Remember what happened downstairs? You have to ask the right question." He put his finger on the glass. "Who was Alf?" Joshua nodded and smiled.

"Yes, I understand." They watched as the glass moved slowly but deliberately to spell out 'Alf was Maureen's lover'. They sat back from the board. "Well, that makes sense, but it doesn't tell me anything. I need to know more about him." They put their fingers back on the glass and Joshua asked, "How did Maureen meet Alf?" The glass spelled out 'In a bank robbery'. They sat back again. "I need to know more." Fingers back on the glass. "When was this?" The glass gave a year, which was the year before Joshua and Jemima were born.

"Right, that all adds up," said Nicholas, taking his finger off the glass. "When did your parents get married?"

"Haven't a clue," replied Joshua.

"What! You don't know your folks' wedding anniversary?"

"17th November. We always get them a card, but I don't know what year. Steph might know – she might have been a bridesmaid or flower girl or something, do you think?"

"Good idea. And Steph knows all sorts of stuff even if she had nothing to do with it. Look, I've been thinking. There are two explanations. Either Aunt Maureen had a fling with Alf, and perhaps Uncle Horace doesn't know you aren't his, or perhaps she was already pregnant before she met Uncle Horace."

"Good thought. You're better at thinking than I am, and we're both better than Jemima." They laughed at this, then Nicholas told him not to be cruel to Jemima. "I do love her, but she's a bit slow sometimes, and it becomes easy to make fun of her."

"But I don't make fun of you."

There was a silence then Joshua said, "Hey, are you saying I'm a bit slow?" Nicholas laughed. "Okay, point taken. Are we going to do more tonight?"

"No. Let's quiz Steph tomorrow. Give us something to work on; might help us ask better questions."

"Fair enough. Good-night."

## Chapter 5

The next morning, they all took part in making breakfast, which was just cereals and toast and marmalade, but there was a better air of co-operation. Jemima gave Noreen and Stephanie a little hug at every opportunity, but the previous night's events weren't mentioned. After breakfast Nicholas announced it was his turn to feed the hens and invited Noreen to give him a hand. This was usually a one-person job, so she knew he wanted to talk to her. It was snowing, but falling gently, unlike the previous day when it was a definite blizzard, so they put their warm coats on and went out. When they reached the hut, they put their hoods down and he fed them while she collected the eggs.

"So what do you want to talk about?" she asked in a whisper.

"It's Steph. Have you noticed? She seems to know what we're doing or talking about even when she isn't in the room."

"I know, and she comes and goes without making a sound. Last night she came into my room without even opening the door!"

"Mine too! You know how my door creaks."

"So does mine. What's happened to her at uni.? She seems to have acquired mystical skills."

"I think Rhonda has something to do with it."

"Rhonda? Who's that?"

"One of the girls she shares the flat with. I've heard her telling Mum about things Rhonda has said and done."

"Things? What things?"

"Rhonda tells her about herbs and stuff, and they make tea and soup with them to cure all sorts of ailments. Sounds to me a bit like potions. You know – hubble, bubble, toil and trouble - and all that."

"You mean Rhonda is teaching her witchcraft? I see what you mean. Not sure if that's cool or not."

"Need to be careful in cased she can hear us. By the way, do you know what year Aunty Maureen and Uncle Horace got married?"

"Haven't a clue," she replied, shaking her head. "Whenever it comes up Mum always changes the subject."

"Hadn't noticed. But you and Mum are more on the same wavelength. Wonder if Steph knows."

"Wonder if Steph knows what?" Stephanie asked, suddenly appearing in the hut.

"You made me jump there! What are you doing out here in the cold without a big coat?"

"Wondered why you were taking so long. Just looking after my favourite brother and sister. If Steph knows what?"

"Do you know what year Uncle Horace and Aunty Maureen married?"

"No, but I'll try to find out."

"How will you do that when all the olds are miles away?"

"Ways and means, children. Ways and means." She turned away from them, gave a knowing wink, and disappeared. Noreen and Nicholas looked at each other in silence for a moment, then she picked up the egg basket and they went back to the house. After lunch Joshua and Noreen loaded up the dishwasher, then the four settled down to a game of Monopoly, but Joshua's mind wasn't really on the game, and he made some poor decisions. After a while they abandoned the game, declaring Noreen the winner as she had so much more money than the others, and they just sat down to read and listen to music.

Up in her room Stephanie was in the lotus position on the floor, with about a dozen scented candles burning and the curtains closed. After about an hour she had settled her mind, and she tried to contact her friend, Rhonda. After two failed attempts Rhonda appeared at the third try, shimmering among the smoke of the candles.

"Thank God for that!" Stephanie exclaimed. "I thought I wasn't going to be able to get you when I actually need you. I managed the other week but that was just for a chat. This time it's important."

"Sorry, darling," said Rhonda. "I've been busy. This sounds urgent. Pray, tell."

Stephanie relayed the story about Joshua and Jemima's father and the upset it had caused, explaining that those who knew were three hundred miles away at a week-long party to celebrate Algernon and Cassandra's wedding.

"Don't worry about that," Rhonda tells her. "That distance isn't a problem. The problem you have is getting into their minds. Try again, but slowly, and concentrate on your mum; you probably have more of an affinity with her. Once you think you have made progress with her, try your aunt. Sorry, dear, I need to go. I'm in the middle of some complicated processes. Goodbye, and good luck." And with that she vanished.

After the evening meal, which was more of a large snack than a meal, Stephanie returned to her room, lit the candles and resumed the lotus position. She concentrated on Mum and tried to put the name 'Alf' into her head. After an hour of getting no reaction, she cleared her mind and tried again, this time working on Aunty Maureen. After another hour of inaction, she settled down with a book until it was time to go to bed. She visited the others briefly to remind them not to stay up too late, but they seemed quite keen on an early night, so she too retired early.

Jemima and Noreen went to sleep quite quickly after a brief chat, but Joshua wasn't ready for sleep.

"I say," he said to Nick after twenty minutes or so of silence, "I would like to take another crack at the board, if you don't mind."

"Depends. What are you after?"

"Well what do you think? More info about Alf. I want to know who he was and what happened to him and stuff like that. If you were in my position, I'm sure you'd want to know too."

"Fair point. But be careful. Let's stick with the idea of me vetting your questions, just in case you get carried away and do something without thinking it through. And I'll have a word with Noreen tomorrow. See what she knows, although it probably won't be much more than I know. But girls talk to their mothers and daughters, so Mum might have let slip something or other."

Joshua agreed and made a list of what he wanted to ask. Nick approved of the list but warned him not to deviate from it. They unboxed the board and put it on the floor, sitting either side. Suddenly they heard Stephanie's voice but couldn't see her. "Be careful, boys," she said.

"Okay, we will," replied Nicholas even though neither could see her. Joshua picked up his list and cleared his throat. They put their fingers on the glass.

"How did Alf die?" Joshua asked. Clearly but not too loudly – he didn't want to disturb the girls. The glass trembled briefly then spelled out 'shot by police'. On to the next question: "Was Mum there at the time?". 'No' came the reply. "Was she pregnant?" 'Yes'. "Did Horace know Mum was pregnant when they married?" 'Yes'. "Did Horace know he wasn't the father?" 'No'. They took their fingers off the glass and sat back.

"Now there's a thing!" said Nicholas. "Do you think she deliberately deceived him, or did she not know either? I mean, she's a bit dizzy at the best of times."

"Yes. I know what you mean. Aunty Maisie is so much more switched on. Sometimes I'm amazed that they're even sisters, let alone twins," said Joshua staring into the distance. "Do you think she knew herself?"

"You mean she didn't know Alf was the father?" Joshua nodded slowly. "Perhaps she didn't. As you said, she is a bit dizzy. There's one way to find out. Do you want to ask the question?"

"Not sure. Can we leave that until tomorrow when you've had an opportunity to quiz Noreen, and see if Steph's come up with anything? Not fully understanding how Steph could find out, but she knows what we're doing even when she isn't in the room, so who can tell? I think we can trust her not to do us any harm, but if I were you, I'd be a bit uncomfortable about not being able to have any personal secrets."

"My thoughts exactly, after what we've learned about her in the last few days."

They put the light off and went to bed, but neither had a comfortable night.

## Chapter 6

In a small castle in a remote part of Scotland the two sisters and Dan were having a whale of a time with friends they hadn't seen for many years. There was a lot of catching up to do, and much laughter about who was fatter or thinner than they used to be, with a few unrecognisable due to make-up and hair colouring. The first day was mainly one for getting used to their rooms, meeting those in neighbouring rooms, and for the drivers having forty winks – it had been a long drive for almost everyone. Then that evening they had a buffet dinner and wandered around, wine glasses in hand, in the dining room, meeting old friends.

The second day was a bit more formal with a sit-down dinner at lunch time, but with plenty of wine and conversations getting louder as more and more wine was consumed. After the meal the guests gathered coffees and teas from a couple of waitresses in the corner of the room and wandered about, talking about jobs and children and where they were all living these days. Meanwhile the servants cleared the big dining table and reorganised the room so that they could have a buffet table at one end and smaller tables dotted about at the other for their evening meal. The walls were lined with comfortable sofas, and the little tables had two or three chairs each, so everyone's needs were catered for. Horace didn't know many people, and didn't really get on with those he did, but he sat in the corner with a few glasses of whisky and ignored the world around him. A few like-minded souls joined him at his little table but said very little. No need to waste time talking when you have a whisky glass in your hand.

Maisie and Maureen had been inseparable, except at bedtime, and there had been such laughter that their sides and jaws ached. Dan had to move away more than once to rest his ears. Then suddenly Maisie froze. She stood completely still, like a statue, and stared across the room, her mouth hanging open but silent for the first time that day.

"Darling, what's wrong?" Maureen asked, concerned.

"Look! Over there! Can't you see him?"

"Where? Who? What am I supposed to be looking at?"

"Can't you see him? It's Alf!"

"Alf? Where?" Maureen followed Maisie's outstretch arm. She went pale and her legs went from under her. Dan was at her side and managed to catch her before she fell. He guided her into a chair and those around fussed over her, fanning her face and offering a glass of water. Hosts Algernon and Cassandra were summoned, and they took charge while Dan shepherded the others away.

"Give her some space! She needs air!" he said while Maisie knelt beside her and stroked her hand. Dan and Algernon helped her to her room, Maisie following on with her bag. They laid her on the bed and left her with Maisie on Maisie's insistence. As Dan was leaving, she called him back.

"What's up, do you think?" he asked. "What's caused this?"

Maisie held a finger to her lips and took Dan to the other side of the room. "She saw someone she hasn't seen for many years," she explained in a whisper.

"Well, yes, but isn't that to be expected here?"

"Not when the person in question has been dead for thirteen years!"

"Who are we talking about here? I haven't seen anyone I know to be dead."

"Go back in and have a look at the guy talking to Marie. They're standing by the piano."

Dan went back to the dining room but returned a few moments later shaking his head. "Never seen him before in my life. Who is he?"

"Never seen him before? It's Alf! Maureen's old boyfriend! You've met him loads of times!"

"I'm going back for another look." He returned twenty minutes later. "No, I've looked at every man in the room. No-one looks even remotely like Alf. He's been dead for years. How could he possibly turn up here?"

Maureen tried to sit up, so Dan went to her side with a glass of water while Maisie went to the other side and propped her up with pillows and cushions. Tears ran down Maureen's face and her expression alternated between horror and disbelief. "Is it him, Maisie?" she asked. "Tell me it's not him. It can't be."

"No, Maureen, it can't be him. He's been dead for fifteen years. It must be someone who looks like him. Try to calm down and have some water. Don't worry. We're here for you. Do you want me to get Horace?"

"Hell, no! He wouldn't understand. I don't think he ever met Alf anyway."

"I think I should let him know. We'll tell him it was just a dizzy turn. Put it down to too much drink. He'll be able to understand that."

"Okay, then, tell him but he doesn't have to come here if he's having a good time. I'd be better with just Maisie, if it's all the same to you."

Dan went to find Horace, but he wasn't really capable of anything. He opened a sleepy eye, flapped a hand and said, "Oh, she's more than capable of looking after herself," had a slurp of his whisky and settled back into his chair. Dan sought out Cassandra and assured her Maureen was in good hands, socialised for a little while, then went back to Maureen's room to find she was feeling a lot better. She was sitting up and having a laugh with Maisie about something.

"I think I'm ready to come back to the party," she said.

"Good, but I would like to know what this is all about," said Dan. "I only met Alf a few times, but I remember what he looks like and I'm certain there's no-one here looks even remotely like him. And he's been dead for more than twelve years."

"Fifteen, actually," said Maisie, "but I saw him too! It was definitely him."

"Did he look like he did last time you saw him?" Dan asked.

"Well, actually, yes, which is a bit strange," she admitted.

"There you go. If it *was* him, he would look fifteen years older, wouldn't he?"

"Well, yes, I suppose he would," said Maisie sheepishly, looking at Maureen, who reluctantly nodded.

"So have you seen a ghost, or have you had too much wine?" Dan asked with a wry smile. The sisters glanced at each other again and giggled, blushing. "Problem solved. Shall we go back?" The sisters nodded, linked arms, and followed him back to the dining room. They both went onto soft drinks for an hour before returning to their favourite tipples.

## Chapter 7

Joshua came down the next morning to find Stephanie already at work making a pot of coffee and boiling the kettle for tea.

"Steph, firstly I want to apologise for being such an arse the other day," he said humbly.

"That's alright," Steph replied graciously. "As long as you don't do it again." He nodded. "And treat your sister with a bit more love and respect." He opened his mouth to speak but thought better of it. "And secondly?"

"Yes, secondly, what can you tell us about life in the family before I came along?"

She sat down at the kitchen table and looked him in the eye. "Sadly, nothing at the moment. I'm trying to find out but failing miserably. I don't remember Alf at all. I was only about four when he died. But I haven't stopped trying. I don't know if it's the weather or because they've had too much wine, but I can't get through to them. I'll try again later."

"What do you mean when you say you can't get through?"

"I'm trying to read their minds. You've probably noticed I know what's going on before people tell me, but Mum and Aunty Maureen, well, at the moment I can't get through."

"Wow! I thought mind reading was just in the films! You can really do it?"

"Yes. How do you think I knew about Alf? Neither you nor Nick had mentioned him to me. Mind you, it isn't easy. It takes a lot of training and practice, especially when the targets are three hundred miles away and drunk. Anyway, the others will be down any minute, so let's press on with breakfast."

"Yes, and thanks for trying to help."

"No problem. I do love you, even though you are an arse at times. And I'm sorry for hitting you so hard. I didn't mean to leave a mark."

Joshua was shocked into silence but soon came round as the others were arriving. Breakfast was a happy meal, with lots of helping each other, and Joshua went out of his way to be kind to Jemima. While Joshua and Jemima were loading up the dishwasher Nicholas had a discrete word with Noreen to find out what she knew about Alf.

"Nothing, I'm afraid. I knew there was something dark about the family's past, but Mum wouldn't let on what it was. I got the impression there was something illegal, but she would never tell me what."

Stephanie returned to her room. "Let's try now before they've had the chance to drink too much," she said to herself as she prepared her room. Seated on the floor, she tried to contact her mother. She knew she had succeeded putting her image into Mum's head but didn't get a reply. She tried a bit harder.

The twins were in the sitting room, huddled around the fire with hot drinks, as the weather had turned cold through the night. They discussed what they knew about Alf, which was very little. Joshua admitted to the girls that Horace didn't know he wasn't their father at the time of his marriage to Maureen, but they agreed they didn't know what he had learned since. Joshua suggested getting the Ouija! Board out again, and the girls looked a bit apprehensive, but while they were debating it Stephanie appeared behind them.

"I'd rather you didn't at the moment. I'm trying to get through to Mum and Aunty Maureen and any psychic waves make it more difficult," she said, before suddenly disappearing. The children sat open-mouthed.

"Did she come in and go out, or did we just imagine it?" asked Joshua.

"I think she just appeared," said Noreen. "I don't think she was actually here."

"Thank goodness for that!" exclaimed Joshua. "Pleased to know it's not just me!" The others laughed weakly, uncertain what to believe. They changed the subject and carried on chatting until it was nearly time for lunch. Noreen got up to start preparing and it and Jemima followed into the kitchen top help.

"Has she done that before?" Jemima asked after a few moments of uncomfortable silence. "I mean the appearing and disappearing thing."

"Good question," Noreen replied. "I haven't noticed it before, but that doesn't mean she hasn't done it. She's been strange ever since she got back from university. She has this friend called Rhonda, and I think they do strange stuff together."

"Do you think it's witchcraft?"

"Could be. Depends how you define witchcraft. Ever since she came back none of us has ever been ill for more than a few hours. If you have a bit of a cold or flu or anything she'll suddenly appear in the room with a hot drink and tells us to drink it, and a few hours later we're cured. But this instant appearing, well, I've just noticed that in the last day or two."

## Chapter 8

Maisie and Dan and Maureen and Horace had just finished a buffet breakfast and had retired to a side table with their coffees. They had an hour or so to kill before they needed to start getting ready for the wedding and smiled and waved and said 'hello' to many friends they hadn't seen for many, many years until the evening meal yesterday. Some they were pleased to see and swapped email addresses and phone numbers, and others they thought 'why did they invite *them*?' They relaxed into the comfy armchairs while the latecomers drifted past, and indicated to the waiting staff whenever they needed a refill of coffee to help keep them awake after a bit too much heavy drinking last night. Suddenly Maisie sat upright and stared at someone on the far side of the room.

"Look!" she exclaimed, pointing, her arm rigid. "It can't be! But it is! It's our Stephanie!"

"Where?" asked Dan, puzzled.

"Over there!" chimed in Maureen. "Can't you see her?"

"Well, actually, no. The woman you're pointing at is, er, can't remember her name, but she does have one. Married to the politician. Can't remember his name either, but she looks absolutely nothing at all like our Steph!"

"Don't you recognise your own daughter? There she is! Oh, she's gone."

"Did you see her, Horace?" Dan asked crossly.

"Good heavens, no, old bean. Neither hide nor hair," he replied without any enthusiasm for the situation. "At this time of day, I haven't had enough to drink for such tomfoolery," he went on, looking at his watch. "Is this PMS, do you think, Dan?"

"No, it most certainly is not PMS, and I don't know about Maureen, but I haven't had a drop to drink yet today – trying to dry out a bit so that I'm lucid for the benefit of my friend Cassandra!" snarled Maisie. "But I definitely saw her, and so did my sister." Maureen nodded in agreement.

Stephanie sat cross-legged on her bedroom floor while the others were busy in the kitchen. It wasn't lunchtime yet, but she set them on early with the preparations, so she didn't need to get involved. She screwed her eyes shut and concentrated until Rhonda appeared in front of her.

"Oh, Rhonda," she exclaimed quietly. "So glad you could make it. I think I've cocked up somewhat, and I might need your help to get out of the mess I've caused."

"Calm down, darling," Rhonda's image replied, shimmering in the candlelight. "Tell me slowly what you've done then we'll see what we can do about it. Start from the beginning. I'm all ears." Rhonda's ears grew and flapped about, as if to make the point. Stephanie giggled and relaxed. She explained about needing to know about Alf, then went on to this morning's event.

"I tried to get inside their heads without mentioning anything, and now they think they saw me at the wedding. Yesterday I was specifically enquiring about Alf, and Aunt Maureen thinks she saw him, but she can be a bit dippy, moreso after drink, but Mum saw him too, but she too had had a lot to drink. That was all laughed off after Dad had calmed them both down, but today they were both sober, and they saw me. Dad didn't, of course, and Uncle Horace, well, he's a bit of a plank so he just dismissed everything Aunty Maureen said, as usual. But the long and the short is that both Mum and Aunty Maureen are convinced they saw me without drink. What can I do to put this right? I don't want them worrying they're having dementia attacks. They're less than fifty!"

"Hmm," said Rhonda, trying not to laugh. "You have got yourself into a plight. But don't fret. We can put this right. I'll try to be a bit more solid – that might make it easier." Rhonda closed her eyes and after about ten minutes sat down on the floor next to Stephanie.

"Wow! You're actually here!" gasped Stephanie, eyes wide open. "I didn't know you could do that!"

"Don't get too excited. I still not actually here. Now, if you try to get into their heads, or perhaps just one to start with, I'll piggy-back in on your thoughts and tell them it's just a dream and to forget it. Does that sound like a plan?"

"Well, yes, as long as you do all the clever stuff."

"Okay. Come on. Let's do it." Rhonda shimmered for a while then reappeared in a quite normal version of herself. Stephanie closed her eyes and concentrated on her mother and aunt. When she opened her eyes she and Rhonda were inside Maureen's head. "This is scary, darling. What a mess! Let's get out and do your mother first." Moments later they were inside Maisie's head. Rhonda spoke gently to Maisie, assuring her that it was all just a dream, and to forget it all. "That's her done. I suggest we go back to your room for a rest before we tackle the other one. Take us away – you're driving."

"Gosh! That really was frightening," said Stephanie as they collapsed in a heap on the floor of the bedroom. The noise brought Noreen up from the kitchen. She knocked on the door then rushed in without waiting for an answer. She stopped abruptly when she saw Rhonda. Noreen was flustered and didn't know what to say, as no-one would be able to get upstairs without going through the sitting room or the kitchen, both of which had been occupied all morning.

"Oh, sorry, Steph. I didn't realise you had a visitor," she said after a brief uncomfortable silence. "We heard a noise, and I came to make sure you had hurt yourself. Are you okay?"

"Oh, er, yes. This is my friend, Rhonda." But Rhonda waved her hand and quickly disappeared. "Oh, she's gone. Never mind."

"Steph, you're scaring me now. What's going on?"

"Er, nothing sweetie. Don't worry. That was Rhonda. She's my friend. Nothing to worry about."

"So where is she now?"

"She wasn't actually here."

"But I saw her with my own eyes!"

"Yes, but when you see someone on TV you don't actually see them, you just see an image. It's a bit like that."

Stephanie had an expression on her face which told Noreen the conversation had ended, so Noreen backed out, closing the door behind her and went back downstairs.

The others were amazed at what Noreen told them and were unsure whether to be scared or fascinated. They sat looking at each other until Stephanie joined them.

"Is lunch ready?" she asked, as though it were just another day.

"Oh, yes, it should be," Jemima stuttered. "Noreen's been teaching me how to cook, so I hope it's okay." She rose and went into the kitchen, followed by Nicholas.

"Teaching her how to cook?" Stephanie asked quietly as soon as they were out of earshot.

"Hardly," said Noreen in a low voice, trying not to laugh. "Explaining the difference between the oven and the microwave for warming things up, and how to use the toaster and grill without burning herself." Stephanie smiled. "But what was going on up there? How did Rhonda get in and out without us seeing her?"

"Like I said. It was like seeing her on TV."

"Okay, we'll leave that for now," butted in Joshua. "What have you been doing? You said you would try to find out what Mum's been up to."

"Let's discuss it over lunch. Jemima's probably got everything on the table by now." They went into the kitchen where Nicholas had set places around the big table and Jemima was very carefully lowering a big casserole dish onto the mat in the middle. Nicholas followed on behind with two plates of garlic bread. "This looks good. Well done, Jemima. Let's tuck in and I'll tell you what I found out. Dish out, please, Noreen." Noreen did as instructed, and they sat around the table, collecting their pieces of garlic bread while Nicholas placed glasses and a jug of water in front of them. After a few mouthfuls Stephanie spoke. "I haven't found out as much as I hoped, but I got a fair bit from Mum. We haven't spent much time in Aunty Maureen's head yet because it's a bit of a scary place. When we arrived, they were both seeing Alf and me all over the place, but we've cured Mum; she thinks it was left over from last night's dream, caused by the drink." She turned to face Jemima and Joshua. "Alf is, or rather was, your biological father. Aunty Maureen was pregnant when she and Uncle Horace married, but he didn't know he wasn't the father, and Aunty Maureen wasn't certain either. Mum and Aunty Maureen worked back to the first time Maureen had sex after her last period, and

Alf was definitely your father, but they didn't work this out until after they had announced her pregnancy a few weeks after the wedding. Uncle Horace thinks you are his, and no-one wants to disabuse him of this. It appears Aunty Maureen always had at least two boyfriends on the go at any one time." She turned back to the group and continued. "Alf was an East End gangster, and the police shot him during an attempted bank robbery. Aunty Maureen was his usual get-away driver, but she wasn't there that day because she was unwell. That's why she survived. So now you know as much as I do. If you want to know more, ask Mum when they get home." Her story telling was over, so she resumed eating. "This is good, Jemima. Well done!" she winked at Noreen and continued the meal. By now the others had finished and they sat back while Noreen served up dessert. After the meal Stephanie declared she needed rest because she and Rhonda intended to try Aunty Maureen the next day. She returned to her room.

The others cleared away the plates into the dishwasher then sat in the sitting room with coffees and teas, wondering what to say. After a while Noreen broke the silence.

"Well, that was a surprise, wasn't it? I knew Mum and Aunty Maureen were quite different but I hadn't realised how much."

"I don't know whether to laugh or cry," said Jemima after another silence. "It's a sad story, but I suppose we are the happy ending. If Mum hadn't felt unwell that day we might have never existed." The others nodded at this. "And Daddy has quite a temper when things don't go his way. What if he'd found out?"

"Well I'm certainly not going to tell him!" said Joshua. They all agreed not to tell anyone they knew this. "So what do you think Steph is going to do next?" he said after another silence.

"Good question, mate," Nicholas replied. "I'm not sure I understand what she's done already."

"It was quite eerie," said Noreen. "When we heard the noise I went in to make sure she was okay. I knocked but didn't wait, in case she was unconscious or something, and there was this Rhonda person, like I said before, just floating. She was obviously cross that I'd seen Rhonda, but it wasn't deliberate. I was concerned. I think Rhonda is some sort of witch, and I think she's teaching Steph to be one too."

"So if Rhonda can come here from far away," said Nicholas thoughtfully, "from Wales or wherever she lives, I suppose Steph can go to the wedding place. I think that's what she did and went into Mum's head to find out all the Alf stuff, but something went wrong, and that's why she sent for Rhonda."

"I think you've hit the nail on the head," replied Joshua.

"She said they needed to go back. Either they've cocked it up and need to straighten it out, or else they need to do Aunty Maureen and couldn't do two in one go," Nicholas continued after some thought.

"Or perhaps both!" said Noreen, alarmed at the idea of things going wrong. "What do you think, Jemima?"

"I don't know what to think. I'm not as clever as you three. I must get my brains from Mummy." They all laughed at this. "But yes, either she's on a repair mission or they haven't started on Mummy yet."

"Let's call it a day for now," suggested Nicholas. "We'll give her time to do something, then question her over the next meal.

## Chapter 9

Stephanie returned to her room and contacted Rhonda, who appeared and sat herself in a chair posture, even though there wasn't a chair there.

"I've told them what we know," she confessed. "It is their parentage, after all."

"Fair enough. But if we're to do the job properly we need to go back and tackle the mad one. Need to straighten her out about the Alf and Steph apparitions. I must admit, your mum has a well-ordered mind. You wouldn't think they were sisters, let alone twins."

"They are twins in many ways, except when it comes to brain power." They both laughed at this.

"Come on, then. This isn't stirring the porridge. Get yourself ready and I'll climb on." Stephanie lit some candles, closed the curtains, and adopted her usual yoga posture. When she was in a trance Rhonda joined her in the ether. "I'm not sure if this is going to be fun or horrendous, dearie, but let's press on; we have to do it. You know the way, and I'm with you."

The wedding ceremony had ended, everyone had glasses of Champagne, and they were filing into the dining room. Maureen was still seeing Alf and Stephanie on lots of people's faces, but Maisie insisted it was left over from a dream caused by too much drink. They sat in their allotted places and their glasses were refilled as soon as they were emptied. Then the food came along. 'Good,' thought Maisie, 'this might soak up some of the alcohol!' The meal was accompanied by several wines, and followed by even more for toasts etc. The staff cleared away everything and rearranged the room ready for partying. The lights were lowered, the disco man started up, and more drink was served. Maureen couldn't stop herself and took advantage of the wines and cocktails. Horace sat in the corner with a glass of whisky while Dan and Maisie entered into the spirit of the day, dancing, drinking and eating for the entire evening.

Stephanie didn't come down for the evening meal, so Noreen took something up on a tray. She knocked and went in. Stephanie was on the floor in the lotus position and didn't respond when Noreen spoke to her. Noreen decided it would be best not to disturb her, so she left the tray on food and drink on a side table and crept out silently. She was explaining this to the others when they heard Stephanie's voice saying "Thank-you." But there was no visual manifestation at all.

"Best leave well alone," said Nicholas quietly. They sat around trying to play Monopoly, but no-one was really concentrating. After a while they decided on an early night. The boys were soon asleep, but the girls chatted for a few hours, Noreen bringing Jemima up to date on the etiquette of boyfriends and couples and other things Jemima should have been told about by her mother, but obviously hadn't.

"All these things to remember," she said, "and with Mummy's brain I'm sure she couldn't."

"Come on, Jemima," replied Noreen. "Some things are just common sense, and some things are just common decency."

"I'm not sure she has enough of either!" They both laughed, and decided enough was enough and went off to sleep.

It was about one o'clock and the party was starting to wind down. Horace stumbled along the corridor, supported by Dan. Maisie and Maureen giggled for the entire walk to their rooms, although neither knew what they were giggling at. When they got there Dan had already put Horace on the bed and removed his tie and shoes. He threw a covering over him and declared he could do no more, as Horace was quite a size. Just then Maureen stumbled in with Maisie trying to keep her upright. They put her on the bed next to Horace and Maisie removed Maureen's shoes and jewellery and loosened her clothing a bit. Their job done they went to their own room, undressed, and had a hug and a snog before getting into bed. A few hours later Maureen awoke. She felt as though something was crawling around inside her head. She was too drunk to get up, and decided to agree with Maisie that it was just the drink. 'If drink can do that to you perhaps I should lay off it a bit,' she thought before passing out again.

Rhonda muttered a few expletives in frustration. "If you kept your room in this state your mum would have a right go at you, and rightly so!" she growled.

"Yes, you're probably right," giggled Stephanie. "But that's not what we're here for. Let's do the business and get out. This place is making me feel ill."

"Yes, that's the state of the place combined with too much drink. I like a good drink, but there are limits."

"I think where Aunty Maureen is concerned there aren't any limits!"

"Well, that's beside the point. You stay here while I poke about to find where these images of you and the bloke are stored." Sometime later Rhonda returned. "I've found them and deleted them, but it wasn't easy. Don't know if I've done any harm or not, but I've done what we had to do. Let's get out of here. This place is a mess the like of such I have never seen before, past, present or future." Stephanie readied herself for the journey and Rhonda locked on to Stephanie's thought stream. Stephanie set off on the journey back, but Rhonda struggled to hang on. "Slow down!" she called out. "Slow down! I'm almost falling off!" The link between their thought streams was unravelling and on more than one occasion Stephanie almost stopped on Rhonda's panicky requests. Then things went wrong in a big way. The link broke and Rhonda spiralled out of control into the blackness. Stephanie felt a sudden jolt as the link collapsed and Rhonda spiralled away, screaming madly. Stephanie followed as quickly as she could but was new to this method of travel and couldn't keep up. She could still see Rhonda but didn't catch up until they were back inside Maureen's head.

Maureen awoke with a jolt. She got up quickly, too quickly, and ended up in a heap on the floor, waking Horace.
"What's going on?" she asked.
"Exactly!" exclaimed Horace. "What's going on? Do you know what time it is?"
"Never mind the time! I've got things in my head! People wandering about doing stuff!"
"Go back to sleep! You're drunk!" He turned over and resumed his snoring. Maureen got to her feet somehow and went to Maisie and Dan's room and hammered on the door. They jumped out of bed and opened it, and a distraught Maureen collapsed into the doorway.

"Help me!" she wailed. "There are people in my head! Get them out!" She lay on the floor, head in hands, and screamed.

"Calm down, darling," said Maisie helping her into a chair while Dan went into the corridor and told the assembled crowd there was nothing to concern them. They went back to their rooms, all but one chap in pyjamas who declared himself to be a psychiatrist and offered to examine Maureen. He returned a moment later with a small bag, and after shining lights into her eyes and talking to her very gently, he said she was in need of urgent psychiatric help. Dan had already roused Horace who came in in a woolly dressing gown.

"We'd better set off back home. Our GP lives not far from us, and he'll come out to see her. He's a pal from the bridge club," said Dan.

"No," interjected Horace. "We pay a small fortune into a private health plan. I want to get value for money out of that. I'll phone them as soon as I'm dressed and see if they have place round here." He disappeared back to their room leaving Maisie and Dan to follow, holding up Maureen. Maisie got her properly dressed, which was quite a struggle as she gave all the appearances of an incapable drunk, while Dan was dressing, then he held onto Maureen while Maisie dressed. After about twenty minutes Horace ended the call. "They have a place about fifty miles away. We need to take her there immediately."

"I'll find Algernon and Cassandra and give our apologies then we can be away," said Dan. "I've started packing the cases; can I leave that for you to finish, darling?"

"Yes. Go and find them. I'll finish ours then give Horace a hand with theirs. She's on the bed mumbling incoherently but I think she's safe to be left as long as someone stays in the room with her."

## Chapter 10

Noreen went up to Stephanie's room, alarmed by the strange shouts she could hear, loud enough to travel to the room below. She knocked but didn't wait for an answer. Two paces in, she stopped. Stephanie was nowhere to be seen. She turned in panic to call Nicholas, then heard a gentle moan from behind the door. Stephanie was there in the corner of the room curled up in a ball. She sent Jemima, who had followed, to alert Nicholas, who was busy in the kitchen.

"I don't know what to do," he said in a concerned voice after examining her briefly. "I didn't want to disturb Mum and Dad, but I think we might have to. But first, let's make her comfortable and see if there's any change over the next hour or so. She's breathing and has a pulse. You never know – it might be just some strange herb she's taken."

"Yes," agreed Noreen. "Rhonda was here the other day, so that could be it. But let's make her comfortable for now, then see if she wants any lunch later." Jemima spread the quilt out on top of a couple of blankets on the floor then Nicholas and Noreen gently lifted their sister out of the corner into the middle of the quilt while Jemima packed pillows and cushions around her so she couldn't roll away. They left her and agreed to come back in a couple of hours. Lunch was a subdued affair. Noreen had gone up to Stephanie's room but there was no change in her condition, so she decided to leave her a bit longer.

"She doesn't seem to be coming to any harm," commented Joshua. "But I think she should show more signs of life than that." The others agreed but decided that while she didn't seem to be unwell they would wait a bit longer.

In Scotland Maisie and Dan had packed all the belongings of both couples and loaded them into the car boot. Horace and Maisie gently lifted Maureen into the back seat where she sat next to Maisie while Dan got into the front to help Horace navigate. They were in quite a snowstorm and sometimes the edge of the road was difficult to see. Algernon and Cassandra and the other guests wished them well and stood in the porch for shelter to see them off until the big car was out of sight. They returned to the dining room where the staff were serving breakfast, but the atmosphere was subdued.

"I don't like these conditions," Horace complained.

"Totally agree," said Dan.

"But this place is only about fifty miles away according to the satnav, but it could take a while in this weather."

"Yes, but take it easy, mate. Better to arrive in one piece than risk an accident."

"Of course, but the psychiatrist chap said she needed help urgently."

Visibility worsened until Dan complained he could hardly see. "I know you're concerned about Maureen; we all are, but I think it might be worth stopping for a short while to see if the storm lets up at all."

"I understand where you're coming from," Horace answered, "But suppose it doesn't – all we've done then is lost time. I want to press on. We'll get there eventually even if it does take an age."

Dan and Maisie agreed reluctantly. Maureen wasn't getting any worse, but she wasn't getting any better either. She moaned continually and intermittently complained about the strange people running around inside her head. Maisie held Maureen's head on her lap and stroked her hair, which sometimes seemed to comfort her, sometimes not.

Suddenly the road seemed to disappear on the left and the car rolled down a steep bank. It rolled over and over about four or five times until it hit a tree and burst into flames. None of them could get out. A few moments later it exploded.

Stephanie let out a blood-curdling scream and her arms and legs flung out so that she was like a starfish laid on the quilt, her eyes staring blankly upward. The others all rushed up to her room and Noreen and Nicholas knelt beside her, shaking her and slapping her face, but she didn't react. After a while she started rocking her head from side to side, calling out to Rhonda. This went on for a few minutes them she screamed again.

"The inside of my head is on fire! Put the flames out! Help me! I'm burning up! Put the fire out!"

Joshua ran out and came back with a jug of water which he threw over Stephanie. It made no difference. She carried on pleading for help, but they didn't know what to do. Nicholas telephoned for an ambulance, but they said it would be two hours before it got there because of the snow. Nicholas tried phoning his parents and Jemima tried hers, but neither got through. Stephanie got more and more agitated and started banging the back of her head on the floor.

"Rhonda!" she shouted. "We've got to get out of this. Aunty Maureen's head is like an inferno and I can't escape!"

At this Jemima burst into tears and ran downstairs; Joshua followed to try to console her. Suddenly Stephanie passed out. Noreen cradled her head in her lap while Nicholas checked for breathing and a pulse.

"She breathing, but very faintly," he said despondently. "She has a pulse but it's very faint and getting slower and slower. It's almost stopped. I think we're going to lose her." A tear ran down his cheek while he put his arm around Noreen, who was weeping copiously. An hour later there was a knock at the door. Two ambulance officers were let in by Joshua who pointed upstairs. They examined Stephanie thoroughly, then shook their heads.

"I'm afraid she's gone," said the young man. "There's nothing we can do for her. It's pointless taking her to the hospital. Meera is contacting control to ask for a doctor to attend to complete the formalities, as we can't take her anywhere because of the weather. Where are her parents?"

"They're at a wedding in Scotland. She's looking after us while they're away," said Nicholas. Meera interrupted.

"The doctor can't get here until tomorrow, Sam. The weather's holding him up."

"Are you the eldest?"

"Yes, by a few minutes over my sister, and by a few weeks over our cousins."

"Cousins?"

"Yes, they're downstairs. Their Mum and our Mum are twin sisters."

"And how old are you, sir?"

"We're all fourteen."

He turned away. "Meera, when you've finished there get in touch with social services. We can't leave minors alone out here with a dead body."

After Meera had contacted them, they started taking their equipment downstairs, when there was another knock at the door. Joshua opened it to reveal two police officers, one male and one female. They removed their hats.

"May we come in?" said the female officers. Joshua nodded and showed them through to the sitting room and invited them to sit.

"May I have a word?" Sam asked the male officer. They went out into the hall and the police officer returned looking grim. Sam shook hands with the children. "We're off to our next emergency. These police officers will look after you. We're sorry about your sister, but there was nothing we could do. She was past the point of no return long before we got here. The doctor's coming tomorrow, but I haven't a clue what time." They left and drove away slowly.

The male police officer gathered everyone together in the sitting room, where Jemima had made tea for everyone. He indicated to them that his female colleague would explain everything. She told them about the crash and informed them that all four were dead. They stayed until a man and a woman arrived from social services. They wanted to take the children away, but they objected strongly. After considering the weather and the time of day they decided to stay the night and see what they could do the next day.

The next morning, just before lunchtime, the doctor arrived to examine Stephanie's body. Everything was just as reported by Sam and Meera, until he examined her head. He shook his head and spoke very quietly to the social services people.

"She's dead; no question, but there seems to be activity inside her head."

He nipped her nose, opened her mouth and tipped her head back. A small cloud of greyish blue smoke drifted out of her mouth into the room. It settled above Stephanie's head and formed into the shape of a woman's head. Noreen, who had been watching, gasped.

"That's Rhonda!" she exclaimed. "That's Stephanie's friend, Rhonda!"

The smoky head turned to face the doctor and said, in a very quiet voice, "Thank-you. Now I can pass over in peace." With that she disappeared. The social services people and the doctor looked at each other in amazement.

# The Dark Side

## Chapter 1

Glen was asleep when the phone rang. Admittedly it was about ten in the morning, but it was still rather unexpected. He reached out to the bedside table to get it before it woke his wife, Brenda. Brenda's job kept her out often until the early hours, so Glen had got into the habit of going to bed when she got in, perhaps three or four in the morning, and getting up late so they could eat and spend time together, ever since he retired.

"Hello, Glen," said the voice at the other end. He recognised it as his old boss, Angus. "Sorry to disturb you, mate, but I need a big favour."

"Hi, Angus. What sort of favour?"

"Well, it isn't actually for me. It's for the government. I need you to do one last job, then I promise we'll never bother you again. I wouldn't ask, but it's pretty important in a really big way. We'll pay you three times what we usually pay, and that's a personal guarantee from me. I told them you wouldn't consider it for the normal rate. Are you game?"

"Depends what it is, Angus. I'm getting on and can't take the stress the way I used to. And after the way they cocked up my final pay packet, well, HMRC got more than I did, a lot more, so I don't want any of that crap this time!"

"So you'll do it. Good man. Can you pop into the office later today?"

"No, I haven't said I'll do it. I'll think about it when I've got details. Yes, I can pop in later today. What is it?"

"Just a trip to the moon. Simple. But you're the only man I can rely on."

"The moon? We're still doing that stuff? I thought Mars was the in thing now. So why do you need me? You've got plenty of younger folk who'd jump at the chance, and you could pay them less."

"Not quite that simple. But we'll talk about that when you get here. Bring Brenda and we'll have dinner after the meeting."

"Sorry, but she has to go to work today. The way things are at the moment she has to book time off two months in advance."

"Okay. Can you be here for one thirty? The government is depending on people like you for your experience and knowledge. That's why we can't use a youngster. It isn't difficult, but we need someone dependable."

At one twenty-five Glen was getting out of his car in the company car park just outside Leicester. The car park men had been warned of his coming and just waived him through with a smile. Glen had always been polite to them, and they appreciated it. He looked around as he walked to the office block. It brought back memories, some good, some not so good, but he was looking forward to seeing his old friend again. Angus was about ten years younger than Glen, and even though his technical skills and knowledge weren't in the same league, he was better at handling the political side of things and had pulled Glen out of a hole on more than one occasion. Angus' elder brother and Glen had been best pals at university, and that's how Glen heard about the job in the first place. He never regretted taking the job, first as a technician on the simulators, then as a space pilot, and several other off-world jobs, before becoming earth-bound as an instructor to the next generation of astronauts. His years up in space were both fun and exciting, but the politics of the organisation had him close to walking out many, many times, but Angus was always there to calm him down and keep the management sweet and calm the troubled waters, often before they became troubled. He strode through the glass doors, showing his pass to the security officer, a small young woman whose smile turned quickly to a frown as soon as she saw the pass.

"I'm sorry, sir, but you can't use that pass here. In fact, I'm going to have to confiscate it." She reached out to take it, but he pulled it away. Her frown turned to a scowl as she grabbed his arm, twisting it behind his back with one hand, and grabbing the pass with the other. She called for assistance, not that she needed it as she already had him pinned to the ground. Two young men came rushing over and took his arms, raising him to a kneeling position while she telephoned reception. "We have an intruder here. He's off to the custody suite."

"No, that might be Dr McManus's visitor. What's his name?"

She looked down at his pass. "Major Glen Pusey, according to his pass, but it's a very old pass. We aren't permitted to admit people with these, and we're told to assume they're up to no good."

"Yes, he's here to see Dr McManus. Bring him to reception and we'll process a new pass for him. He's going to be with us for a few weeks, possibly longer."

The officer called to her colleagues, who brought Glen back and released him at the reception desk. They were full of apologies, but Glen wasn't impressed. He grudgingly completed the form at the reception desk, by which time Angus had emerged from the lift.

"How to win friends and influence people. Title of a book. Your people need to read it."

"Sorry, Glen. This wouldn't have happened if you hadn't tried to use your old pass."

"But when I tried to hand it in ten years ago, *you* told me to keep it in case it proved useful. Next time I'll just hand it in, and if they won't accept it, I'll burn it."

They stepped into the lift together. "Never mind that now. We've important stuff to discuss. Have you had lunch yet?"

"I had a small bite to eat before I set out."

"I haven't had mine yet. Do you want something light?" Glen nodded. They arrived at the top floor and Angus ordered food and drink as they passed a young man at a desk. In the office they sat on a comfy sofa and discussed pleasantries until the food arrived. "Thanks, Geoff. Please make sure we aren't disturbed for the next two hours." The man nodded and left.

"This place isn't as friendly as I remember it," said Glen with a grimace.

"Sorry about that. Security is much tighter now that there's so much international conflict. In the old days they thought the Brits were just doing it for fun. Now they know that we mean business and we get about three attempts a week at infiltration by foreigners of one form or another. Anyway, about the job. It isn't difficult for a man of your abilities. It's a trip to the moon, a few experiments when you get there, then coming home. Two weeks maximum. If the experiments go well, it could be ten days."

There was a silence while Glen stared into the distance. He looked back at Angus who smiled broadly, then out of the window across the flat countryside. Eventually he looked back at Angus. "So what's the catch? Why me for such a simple job? What's so special about this? If you don't tell me, and I mean tell me everything, I'll just walk out and never darken your doors again. Professionally, I mean. You and Jean will always be welcome for dinner."

"Okay. I understand you don't trust the old firm. Sometimes I don't either, but they pay well. This job is for a new project. It sounds simple, but there are complications. It involves landing on the dark side of the moon – the side that's always turned away from Earth. The problem there is that you can't send a direct radio signal from there to here with any sort of reliability. There will be another ship at right angles to act as a relay. You will send your signal to them, and they'll bounce it to us here. There'll be a third ship, and perhaps a fourth, to interrupt the signal so that it appears to be millions of miles away, and the object is to work out what we need to do to make it work with a one hundred percent reliability. It's for our next Mars trip. We've been to Mars before, but every time the signal disappears for weeks at a time while we're on opposite sides of the sun. Sometimes it doesn't disappear completely, but becomes unreliable, and I mean *very* unreliable. Our plan is for our Mars base to be the centre of a colony, rather than just an engineering and exploration outpost. The security issue is that other nations, Russia, India, Australia, and even USA are keen for us to do all the work then walk off with our know-how without paying a penny for one thing, and perhaps using it for military purposes for another."

Glen sat back and thought for a moment. "Yes, that all makes sense, but why me? Surely your young astronauts could do the job just as well without needing to have big money thrown at them."

"Hmff! Yes, we've got plenty of them, but three of them came home from their hols with Covid, didn't tell anyone, and now more than half the operational workforce have it."

"Covid? I thought that was a thing of the past!"

"So did we, and in this country it is. But they go abroad to less well-developed places like Italy and Turkey and here we are."

"Italy?"

"Yes. Their right-wing government isn't interested in such things. If you get it, well, it's your own fault. That's how they see it. And as for Turkey, don't get me started. So that's why we need to come to people like you. We know that if you *have* been abroad, you'd take precautions."

"I see. Well, Brenda and I always do the test as soon as we get back, but it's always negative, and we just do that to keep the insurance policy valid. So has your pool of reliable people really shrunk that much?"

"Yes. I shouldn't tell you this, but if you turn us down, I have another three people to call on, none of them anywhere near as good as you, or else we cancel the project, and the government and our sponsors will be up in arms. In a big way."

"Well, that explains why I come at such a high price."

"Exactly."

"Obviously I need to discuss this with Brenda, but I can't see her objecting. There's nothing dangerous. A simple moon trip, and the money will mean she can retire. I mean, in theory she already can, but our younger daughter is in financial difficulty and we're helping her out until her divorce comes through. That's the only reason Brenda's still at work. I had to stop when I did for health reasons, but Brenda's always been healthy."

"Sorry about that. If you hadn't been on the premises the day of the explosion you could have carried on too."

"Assume I'm saying yes, but as a favour to you, and to Brenda of course. Not out of any loyalty to the firm. I got no help when they decided to line the tax man's pocket with *my* money."

## Chapter 2

The telephone rang and was answered by Julian. He stuck his head round the office door of the Foreign Secretary. "Sir, switchboard have Mr Adams on the line. He's the Secretary of State."

"I know who Mr Adams is, Julian. Tell them to put him through. Thank-you."

Gilbert settled himself at his desk; talking to Adams was never comfortable. He let the phone ring three times before answering it. No need to appear too eager to the Americans. They generally feel too eager to start with – must be too much sugar or food colouring or something.

"Hello, Gene. Good to hear from you. What brings you to phone me at this time of the day? It must be middle of the night for you."

"Gilbert, we need to talk, and not on the telephone. I don't trust them."

"I quite understand that. I don't trust yours either."

"What? Anyhow, I need to face-to-face you about sumpen important. Will you be around at, say, three today?"

"Well, actually yes, but how will you get here by then?"

"Details, man. I'm already here. I'll come to your back door dressed casual like some casual visitor."

"No, casual visitors would come to the front door. So where are you now?"

"If I comes to the front, I'll have to say who I am, and they'll know I'm here."

"So where are you now?"

"Don't tell nobody, but I'm in the Thames. You know, the big river. Tell you what. I'll meet you at Charing Cross Station by the doughnut stand and we'll find a quiet spot. I'll buy you lunch at McDonalds and we can eat in one of your gorgeous parks."

"Oh, alright. See you there at three. But what are you doing in the Thames? I mean, I don't suppose for a moment you're swimming, and I didn't even know you were over here."

"Oh, er, I'll explain later. See you at three. Come alone and make sure you ain't followed."

Just before three o'clock Gilbert made his way to Charing Cross Station and approached the doughnut stand. Gene was already there, with his hat pulled down over his eyes and a newspaper covering part of his face. When he saw Gilbert, he smiled and tucked the newspaper under his arm. They greeted each other warmly and Gene led the way to McDonalds. He ordered two Big Mac meals, much to Gilbert's disdain, and as he paid for them the man held onto the bags, looked him squarely in the eye and asked, "Are you taking away, Sir?"

"Sure am, boy."

"Far, far away, Sir?"

"Far, far away – thanks."

He took the bags with one hand and grabbed Gilbert with the other. "Come on, we gotta move," he said as he pulled Gilbert along behind, looking around as they went. They went out of the station and hailed a cab. "Head for Regent Street," he told the driver. "Take the next left, then left again." The driver followed the instructions. "Okay, stop here." They got out and he gave the driver a handful of notes and set off at speed with Gilbert struggling to keep up. He led them to what looked like the rear entrance of a hotel and knocked on the door in a pattern, as though it were morse code or something. The door opened and they were both dragged in.

"This isn't one of our 'gorgeous parks', old bean."

"Change of plan. We were being followed."

"How did you know that?"

"The burger boy told me."

They were shown into a pleasant room with sofas and a coffee table, and they settled down to eat.

"Why would they be following you? Are you up to something?"

"Hey, we are the US of A. We're always up to sumpen, but they think we're up to sumpen bigger than normal."

"They?"

"Dunno. Could be anybody. But when you're dead it don't matter who."

Gilbert chewed thoughtfully on his burger, then looked up at Gene. "Gene, we've always been straight with each other, so I want you to be straight with me now. One, what were you doing in the Thames, and two, what do you want to talk to me about that is so secret?"

Gene got up and walked to a little bookcase. There was a radio there, which he turned on and turned the volume up.

"Sorry, bud, but sometimes I don't even trust our own guys." Gilbert nodded his understanding. "Point one, I have a little office in the river, which I use now and then, for instance, when I have to buy my daughter a present from Harrods or some place. I use it for business too, of course, when I need to be here secretive like."

"Oh, I see. Secretive. Like now, you mean."

"You got it, bud. And point two, we hear you doing a moon shot. Yeah?"

"Well, I believe there's something of that nature in the offing, but I can't give details."

"Well neither can I, but we know it's connected to your Mars shot, and we know yous guys are going to the wrong side of the moon. The dark side – is that what you call it? I never understood why you always calls things by the wrong words."

"I haven't been fully briefed, but I gather that's the gist of it. Why is that a problem for you?"

"It ain't no problem for us. It's just what you might find there. We don't want you guys blabbing to the papers and the TV if you find something, er, let's call it unexpected."

"Unexpected? In what way?"

Gene shuffled in his seat uncomfortably. "Don't tell nobody what don't need to know, but there's remains."

"Remains?"

"Remains. Crashed ships, dead bodies, stuff like that."

"Oh, I see. That sounds rather unfortunate. But we never heard of anything like that, failed missions, I mean."

"Exactly. Do you remember Apollo thirteen?"

"Well, yes, but you got your chaps back safely."

"Yeah, but the Ruskies had a good laugh at us over that. Ever since then we haven't announced any missions until after they got back. No more failed missions. You got it?"

"Oh, I see. So you send a crew up on, let's say 1st July, and they come back on, say, 10th July, and you advertise it as going on 11th and returning safely on 21st. And if they don't come back you keep stumm, as though they never went. Is that about it?"

"You got it, bud. That's exactly it. So no more failed missions for the Ruskies to laugh at. Or the Chinese or nobody else."

"So you had a failed mission and we'll find it, and you don't want us to tell anyone. Yes?"

"Don't tell nobody."

"Okay. Just one thing."

"What's that?"

"Your office in the Thames. Do you have some sort of underground hideaway?"

Gene sighed and looked embarrassed. "You got me on that one. We have a little boat out there near our embassy."

"Little boat? Just where, exactly? Our people haven't reported any American boat."

"Well, your guys might not have seen it."

"And why is that? Is it in disguise?"

"No, it ain't."

"Don't tell me it's a submarine. Is it?"

"Well, yeah, but just a little one."

"You've got a submarine moored in the Thames without our knowledge! No doubt without our permission either! Gene, this could cause a diplomatic scandal of immense proportions!"

"Which is why it's got to stay our secret. Look, I've fessed up about our biggest embarrassment, so in return I need you to keep stumm about this. I owe you a favour, and we both owe it to our governments to keep this secret a secret. Okay?"

"Okay. You owe me a favour. A big one."

## Chapter 3

Glen arrived at the Lackenby launch pad. Lift off wasn't for a few days. But he needed to complete some training and the final medical checks and meet the other astronauts. All the paperwork had been completed, and the aim of the project had been sketched out in broad brush terms, but there was no detail about any aspect of the trip. He was shown into the training suite which was an 'all-in-one-room' facility so that top secret jobs weren't in danger of being compromised by visits to toilet facilities or movement between rooms. He had spent many days in here, some happy, so less so, and he was familiar with everything despite the number of years since he last visited. He was the first to arrive and helped himself to coffee and biscuits and made himself comfortable on the sofa in the corner. He was puzzled at the location. Why Lackenby? Leicester had always been the main launchpad, and Lackenby, near the coast, was only used for small launches, usually unmanned, but its location was useful for debriefing after recovery from the North Sea, and it was ideal for training, as those who failed to qualify for a project were kept well away from the main sites near Leicester and Milton Keynes. Still, it was an easier journey for him. Next to arrive were Sonya and Gloria who had arrived the previous day and stayed in the accommodation suite. They knew each other well, having started together and had been trained by Glen shortly before his retirement. In their early days they giggled a lot, and Glen wondered if they still did.

"Well, hello!" Glen greeted them with a big smile, which they returned enthusiastically. "Didn't expect to see you two."

"Didn't expect to see you either," said Gloria. "Our old teacher brought out of retirement! What are you teaching us this time?"

"No, not teaching. Being taught." He smiled again as their eyes opened wide.

"What, are you coming with us?" said Sonya, astounded. "On a mission? Wow! We *are* honoured." They helped themselves to coffee and biscuits and sat at the coffee table opposite Glen.

"Angus hasn't given me the full brief yet, so I don't really know what's what."

"Angus! Hey, Sonya, we're in with the big boys on this one!" said Gloria.

Sonya lent forward holding her mug of coffee in both hands and looked serious. "They pull you out of retirement and you don't know what's what? I wouldn't be comfortable if I were you," she said.

"Got to admit, I'm not," he said sitting back. "What can you two tell me?"

"Very little," said Gloria. "We are the relay ship. Our moon ship lands on the dark side and we are out at an angle bouncing comms back and forth between the moon ship and here. We haven't been told how or why."

"That's pretty much what I know. Do you know about the intercept ship?"

"The what?"

"The intercept – it interferes with the signal to make it look as though it's travelled a few million miles." Gloria and Sonya looked at each other open-mouthed.

"Er, no," said Sonya. "We thought it sounded too easy. What's all that about?"

"That's to simulate the Mars project. So that signals can get through when Mars and Earth are on opposite sides of the sun. But I've probably said too much already." They stopped talking as they heard the door open behind them. Angus came in.

"Ah!" he said. "Old friends getting together."

"Yes, Glen was our first instructor when we started here all those years ago, but it was in Milton Keynes in those days," said Gloria with a smile.

"Good. I'm pleased to see you getting on well. Lackenby has been a better option ever since Covid trashed our schedules, so here you are. Today I'm here to fill in any gaps in your knowledge of the project and answer any questions. Up to a point, you understand. Then you'll spend most of tomorrow and the day after on the final medicals and final briefings and we launch two days later." He looked at his watch. "We're waiting for the intercept crews to arrive then we can start." The door opened and four young men came in. "Ah good. Here they are. We'll just spend a few moments for tea and biscuits then we can start. I've ordered a proper breakfast for ten fifteen. This is Faruk, Dominic, Ivor and Seamus. Meet Gloria, Sonya and Glen. Time to chat later. Get your drinks and let's sit round the conference table over there."

Armed with coffee and biscuits they gathered round the table and listened intently as Angus took them through the nuts and bolts of the project. The main objective was to test the ability to bounce the signal off the relay ship without too much drop in quality, then when that was working satisfactorily, to introduce the intercept ships, one at a time, to simulate the signal travelling two hundred and fifty million miles, give or take several thousand, as that would be the approximate distance when Earth and Mars were on opposite sides of the sun. If this worked it would be a big step to establishing a permanent base on Mars, which could be used as an engineering location for future projects, with a possible view to establishing a self-sustaining colony in the more distant future.

"This is even more top secret than usual. No-one else knows we're doing this. The Americans have a vague idea, but they don't know why. Our government is thinking that even if we don't use it ourselves, we can sell it for megabucks. That's why up to now you've only known about your part in it. Today is the first time I've explained the whole thing to anyone below the level of cabinet minister or the top chaps in the armed forces. Any question?"

A few hands went up, and Dominic asked his question, which was the same question the others had. Angus asked for silence while breakfast was delivered, which the catering staff were used to, so that being ignored didn't upset them. Over breakfast Angus fielded a few more questions which were much lower level, then he gave out the info packs. "These should tell you everything else you need to know, and time has been allocated for them to be read while you're in the queue for the medics tomorrow."

"Just one more thing," said Glen. "Am I alone on this? I mean, I'm as good a pilot as the next person, but I've always gone up in a crew of two or more. I thought solo flights weren't permitted."

"Good point," said Angus looking uncomfortable. "There's a good reason for this, but I'm not allowed to tell. Personally, I agree with you, but that decision is out of my hands. We had a pilot allocated, but it was all changed at the last minute." There was general disgruntlement at this.

"Gloria and I are both qualified pilots, and both qualified comms engineers, so that if anything happened to one of us the other could take over. I wouldn't be happy if I were Glen at the moment," said Sonya, to grunts of agreement from the others.

Angus shook his head. "As I said, not my decision. I'm not in favour, but those upstairs pointed out that Glen is our most experienced operative and should be able to manage. Just need to hope there's no illness or accident while he's up there." More grunts of disquiet. Angus held his hands up. "I know, but as I said, not my decision. Let's move on. Glen goes up in two days' time. Gloria and Sonya go up later the same day, and the interceptor ships the following day, you, Faruk and Seamus at eleven o'clock, and you, Dominic and Ivor at five o'clock. All this is documented in your info packs which also tell you when to go for your medicals, when to eat and when to sleep, when to pee and when to poo, you know, the usual crap." This eased the tension a bit. Angus finished eating, had another coffee, and shook their hands before leaving. They sat in silence for a minute or so, then introduced themselves more thoroughly to those they didn't already know.

"I'm a bit suspicious about this, Glen," said Gloria when they had settled down with more coffee.

"Me too," replied Glen. "They bring me out of retirement, send me up alone, and involve Angus, who's just about the most senior guy in the organisation apart from the directors. There's something fishy about this."

Dominic had been sitting in silence reading the info pack while the others were chatting. "I see your point, Gloria. I've skimmed through this and there's nothing difficult or complicated. It looks to me like they're putting an unnecessary level of seniority into this, and I can't figure out why."

"Proverbial sledgehammer to crack the proverbial nut," quipped Seamus with a grin. The others agreed.

## Chapter 4

The day of the launch of Glen's ship arrived and he was up early and cleaning his teeth when there was a knock at the door. He made sure he was decent and went to answer it. It was Angus, fully dressed in suit and tie, as usual. They were old friends, so Glen assumed this was just to bid farewell and wish him good luck, but Angus had a serious expression on his face.

"May I come in?" he asked.

"Of course," Glen replied, offering him the chair. The accommodation units were sparsely furnished as visitors weren't permitted. But Angus was the boss, so he could break the rules if there was good enough reason.

"Sorry to bother you before breakfast, but I want to be totally straight with you, and I would get into trouble if they knew I was here." He looked around the room. "Can't see any cameras or microphones, but I'd be surprised if there aren't any. But I don't care. They can sack me if they want. I owe it to you as a friend."

"Look, I appreciate your honesty, but I don't want to get you into any grief," Glen replied, seating himself on the edge of the bed.

"No, don't worry about that. As I said, they probably know I'm here already. No, the thing is I've just had a call from the operations director, who's just had a call from the Foreign Secretary. When you get there, you might find, er, some unexpected stuff. Whatever you do, you mustn't mention it to anyone. Not in person, most definitely not on the radio, not at all by any means. The things you might find are remnants of a moonshot by the Yanks three or four years ago."

"I didn't know they'd been to the dark side. So will there be equipment and stuff?"

"Yes, er, lots of equipment, and er, bodies. Dead bodies in space suits." Glen didn't know what to say. His mouth opened and closed but no sound came out. "Yes, that's how I felt when they told me. The trip didn't make it to the news, because they only publicise successful missions. The ship went up and never came back. They know it landed safely, but that's all they know. It might have taken off and they lost control, but it's more likely it never left the moon."

"Wow. Is that why I'm going alone?"

"Not exactly. The man who was to go up with you, well, someone decided he was a security risk. Don't ask how or why, because I haven't a clue, but he was taken off the project and they couldn't get a replacement ready in time. If the men got out of their space suits there'll be no deterioration as there's no atmosphere, so they'll look like live bodies, but don't be fooled. My advice is not to touch anything, just in case. You never know what bugs might be there from meteorites or whatever, or from anything the Ruskies left behind. We know they've been there, but we don't know why or what they did."

"Well, thanks for the warning."

"They didn't want me to tell you. My conscience wouldn't let me keep quiet. Good luck, mate. See you in a couple of weeks."

They stood and shook hands, then hugged briefly. Angus left. Glen sat for a few moments then he finished getting ready and went to the communal area for breakfast. He ate in silence. The others sat silently too, then wished each other good luck. A few hours later he was in his space suit and on his way to the ship.

The launch was successful, as was the launch of the relay ship a few hours later. When Glen was in lunar orbit, he contacted Gloria and Sonya in the relay ship. Both ships had had good journeys and arrived in position bang on time. Glen had been worrying about what Angus had said during quiet moments when the auto pilot was in control, but at other times he had to concentrate on what was happening. Eventually both ships reached the desired position for trial transmissions, and the first transmission reached the relay ship perfectly. After a series of successful tests, they repeated the exercises but with the relay ship bouncing them directly to earth without intercepting.

The next day the interference simulation ships were in position, so they repeated everything with one 'getting in the way' again without any difficulties, then with both interference ships. With both in position the signal needed to be boosted by the relay ship, and, apart from taking twenty-three minutes instead of four, which was what they expected, everything was fine.

Now to repeat it all from the surface. Glenn was an experienced pilot, and some of the manoeuvres were carried out by autopilot anyway, so the following day saw his ship land on the dark side of the moon completely successfully and precisely at the desired place and at the desired time. Sonya passed all this down to Mission Control in Lackenby and messages of congratulations came back from Earth. Glenn made the usual tests for radiation levels etc., then disembarked and unloaded the transmission station parts. This took quite a while, so after unloading he had a meal and a sleep. On the next 'morning', which wasn't actually a morning, he had breakfast then built the station. It would have been much easier with an extra pair of hands, but that was an option he didn't have. A few hours later the station and the power unit were in place, and he connected them together. With the power unit in place, he could turn on a brighter light which lit up the whole area rather than just the few yards around the station previously illuminated by the ship's lights. Looking around, he saw something that made him stop in his tracks. About fifty yards away was an astronaut in a space suit.

## Chapter 5

Glen walked slowly towards the astronaut and stopped about three yards away. There was no movement from it. He didn't expect any. Angus had warned him there might be dead bodies, but he expected them to be laid flat on the ground rather than stood bolt upright. And then he noticed the astronaut was facing at right angles to him, whereas it had been facing away when he first spotted it. Could it have moved? Surely not. No, he must have walked in a curved path. But how did he do that? He glanced back to his own ship and the transmission equipment, and no, he had walked in a straight line. So what was going on? Never mind. Perhaps the situation was twisting his thoughts. Behind the astronaut were bits of wreckage, some bearing the USA flag, and further afield was a spaceship with a big gaping hole where part of one side had blown off. Glen slowly, very slowly, approached the astronaut, and when he was quite close, he spotted a control panel with a few lights blinking in a pattern. Closer inspection revealed a few instructions and two buttons marked 'reset'. He didn't know what to do. UK space suits didn't have anything like this. They did have reset buttons, but not overtly marked, and certainly not with instructions the casual passing untrained astronaut could follow. What should he do? He couldn't see through the visor, but that was to be expected, as the visors were heavily tinted to keep unwanted radiation out. He left the space suit and walked on to the damaged spaceship. It looked as though it had been hit by something, perhaps some space debris such as a meteorite, or a piece of junk from another spaceship. When he got closer, he found a space suit on the ground with half of one side ripped away. He climbed the steps into the ship and peered inside. There were bits of control panel and other equipment hanging out of place, but no signs of personnel. Going back to the space suit laid on the ground he pulled it open to see what condition the astronaut was in. Obviously he was dead, and the left arm was hanging off, the eyes were bulging, as would be expected after a sudden decompression caused by exposure to the vacuum of space, and he had a terrified expression on his face. There was no sign of decay, but again, this was to be expected in the silence of space with no air or moisture. Glen sighed and decided to give the man a decent burial. Inside the ship was a spade, and he managed to dig a hole quite quickly in the soft soil, which was more like dust than normal soil. He removed the man from his suit and gently placed him in the hole and covered him up. He said a short prayer and returned to his own ship. It was almost time for the first set of test transmissions, so he had a bite to eat and readied himself and the equipment. Managing the transmission station was a bit more difficult than transmitting from inside the ship, as no matter how he moved things, the sun's reflected glare always made some control panel or another awkward to read. Why hadn't they thought of this when they designed it? Eventually he managed to position a sheet of obscured perspex to dampen the glare, except that made some panels too difficult to read. But, not one to give up, Glen set up some torches on stands, and everything worked. He made the transmissions, and Gloria confirmed they had been received successfully, followed by a bit of a wait until Lackenby confirmed reception, with and without the interferences from the other ships. Ten out of ten for part one. All he had to do now was wait until the moon had moved round a bit and repeat everything. This gave him about eight hours to fill, so he had his next meal, then went back to the dead space suit standing alone in the dust. He read the 'restart' instructions again. Sounded simple enough. But why would they be printed on the space suit? Well, the Americans do things like that, mainly because they aren't like us. Anyway, the question in Glen's mind was whether it was safe to do it. He began to doubt his own sanity – the space suit had been there at least three years, from what Angus had said, so there wasn't any harm giving it a go. But was there any point? He checked his timings. He had another three hours before his next transmission, and he'd had a meal quite recently. Yes, let's try it. He followed the instructions – hold down the two 'Reset' buttons together and press the red 'Go' button about a foot away. He did this, and released them, and stood back. Nothing happened. Well, what a surprise! The suit had enough power to flicker a few little LED lights, but not enough for anything else. He was turning away when he saw a new light out of the corner of his eye. He turned back to see a display panel showing the words 'need more energy' in red. He returned to the transmission station and came back with the trolley he had used to move everything from the ship to the transmission site. He loaded the space suit onto it, which was surprisingly light considering it contained a body, and trundled it back to the ship. The winch helped him get it inside, and the put it into the co-pilot's chair. He had a power cable, which he used to charge up various small tools, and after a bit of searching he found the power socket on the suit. He plugged it in, turned it on, and sat back, expecting nothing significant to happen. Some of the lights on the control panel began to pulsate, and he could hear a humming sound. Glen wondered what to do. Should he disconnect it? He was about to try to remove the cable when he heard a voice. It was coming from the ship's sound system, the system used to communicate with earth and the other ships.

"Thank-you," it said in an electronic monotone.

"Er, are you okay in there?" he asked.

"I am charging up," said the suit.

"You can remove your helmet. The air is pure and adjusted to be the right mixture for us."

"No. Helmet must remain."

"Are you sure? It must be rather warm in there now."

"Must remain on."

"How long have you been in there?"

"Approximately fifty-three million years."

"You've obviously got a problem. Is that from memory or did you calculate it? No, but honestly, mate, how long have you been in there? I mean, how long since the accident?"

"Accident? No accident. I have been on this moon fifty-three million years. I have been in this spacesuit three years, fourteen months and two days."

Glen began to think the astronaut was losing his marbles. Not surprising after such a long isolation. "So what's your name?"

"Name? No name."

"Come on, pal. Let's get you out of there and you'll feel better for some cooler air." He reached forward to remove the helmet, and the astronaut's arm suddenly swung up and knocked Glen off his feet.

"Hey! No need for that! But you're on my ship now, so I have a right to check you for the safety of the ship and the crew, and a duty to look after your health and wellbeing. Come on, I'm going to take your helmet off. UK Regulations."

"Must comply with regulations." The astronaut lowered his arm and sat passively.

Glen had been wondering which direction to take the situation, but now he became concerned. An American astronaut wouldn't be so compliant. All the Americans he had worked with in the past, and there had been quite a few during the years of the Joint Space Venture programmes, would have said, 'I don't do UK regulations; I'm an American citizen!' or some similar outburst. At this point Glen began to seriously doubt his own sanity. Here he was talking to an astronaut who should have been dead for the last three years and talking about regulations in order to pull rank. He sat and pondered his options. Well, best foot forward. He unclipped the helmet and began to unscrew it when the astronaut's arm came up again and grabbed Glen's arm.

"Must not remove helmet. Health and safety. Must stay on."

Glen pushed the arm away rather roughly and quickly finished unscrewing before the man had a chance to stop him. He was very strong, but not very quick, so the helmet came off in a matter of seconds. It fell to the floor and Glen's mouth dropped open. There was nothing there.

## Chapter 6

Glen didn't know what to do. He looked down into the space suit and saw nothing. He picked up the helmet and put it in the corner out of the way, then turned back to the empty suit.

"Who are you? *What* are you?" he asked slowly. He carefully disconnected the power cable when it wasn't watching. Wasn't watching? It didn't appear to have any eyes, so how could it watch? Or was it 'sensing' his whereabouts some other way?

"Do not do that," said the suit. "Need power." Its gloved hand grabbed Glen's arm and held it tightly. "Need power." Glen struggled to get free but couldn't. "Need power," it repeated. Should Glen hold out against it, assuming that when its power levels got low enough, he would be able to break free? Or would that take too long, as at the moment he couldn't reach his food or water, or any control panels? Or should he reconnect the suit, which he could do with his free hand, assume it will cooperate, and try again to get the upper hand once he had time to arrange essential items more conveniently nearby? Making sure he was as far away from the suit as he could get, which wasn't easy in such a small space, he decided to question it.

"How did you get here? How did you end up like this? How have you survived?"

"I came by spaceship, like you did. Our ship was hit by a meteorite. I haven't survived – I am dead, but my life force continues in this suit. One day you will be like me."

"So you are a ghost?" Brief silence.

"That's what you would call me."

They sat in silence for some minutes while Glen considered the situation and his next course of action.

"Need power," it said after a while. That gave Glen a bargaining tool.

"If I plug you in, will you release your grip on my arm?"

"Yes." After its previous honesty Glen decided it wasn't capable of telling a lie. He reconnected the power cable, and it immediately released his arm. He quickly took on board some food and drink, then turned to the main control panel. "You can't use that," said the voice. "It doesn't work I have disabled it." Glen turned away from the panel after trying a few basic functions.

"Now look here!" he said sternly. "You can't do this! This is His Majesty's Spaceship, and as the senior officer on board I am responsible for making sure regulations are followed."

The suit clicked and whirred for a moment or two before speaking again. "You have no regulation about disabling the control panel," it said.

Glen was dumbfounded. It was right. 'Do not disable the control panel' was never mentioned in training and didn't appear in the manuals. "Why have you disabled them?" he asked.

"To stop you using them."

"Why do you want to stop me?"

"I am summoning my colleagues and you would try to stop me doing that."

"Colleagues? What colleagues? How many? Where from? I want to know what's going on!"

"I need them here so that our combined power can fulfil our destiny. You must not stop us. We want revenge on your leaders for destroying our community."

"Just a minute," said Glen, struggling to take it all in. "What are you talking about? When did our leaders destroy your community? You seem quite strong and clever, so I don't understand how we could do it."

"We have gained strength and knowledge here waiting for the opportunity. I have learned a lot in three years, fourteen months and two days, and we share our knowledge. We are a collective."

"So your colleagues are on their way here now?"

"Correct."

"Then what?"

"Then we take our revenge."

Gene Adams was in bed with his wife. It was a big bed and there was plenty of space between them, which was just as well as he had been tossing and turning for several days. Mrs Adams was fast asleep. She always slept in an eye shade and ear plugs because her husband liked to read in bed, and almost every night snored like a buffalo in labour. Gene had slept fitfully ever since his last visit to London, England. It seemed the right thing to do at the time, but the more he thought about it the more uncomfortable he became. He wished he hadn't said so much to Gilbert. Gilbert was a foreign power. He was a friendly foreign power, and an important ally, but he was still a foreign power. Keeping the UK of GB sweet was an important part of his job, but disclosing government secrets to a foreign power definitely wasn't. He awoke at about six o'clock with a feeling there was someone in the room. He reached for his bed-side drawer, trying to be silent, and pulled out his Colt 45. He clicked the bedside lamp on and looked around the room, moving as little as possible, and despite his best efforts let out an audible gasp at what he saw. There at the foot of the bed looking straight at him stood what looked like an astronaut in full space suit.

"Who are you?" he hissed in a loud whisper. "What are you doing here? I have a gun and I'm not afraid to use it."

"I am here for you," the astronaut replied in a monotone electronic voice. "I am here for revenge."

Gene sat up but carried on pointing the gun at the astronaut. "Revenge? What have I done to you?"

"To me and my people, nothing. But to your own people, you sent them to their deaths, you and your government and your nation, and never acknowledged their sacrifice, never treated their remains with respect."

"I don't understand. And if I did nothing to you, why are you here for revenge?"

"You sent people to their deaths on the moon, on Mars and other places, and never acknowledged their fates. I am here to stop you doing it again. Then when you are dealt with, we will stop your race doing it again. I am here to kill you, then we will destroy the human race."

Gene raised his gun and fired at the astronaut, one bullet in the chest and another in the head. The astronaut disappeared, revealing two bullet holes in the full-length mirror he had been standing in front of. Blood trickled down the mirror from the bullet holes. He put his hand out to his wife, wondering how she hadn't been wakened. He felt something wet, and staring at his wet hand, saw blood running down it, down his arm, and onto the bedding.

Esther was in the kitchen preparing breakfast for Mr and Mrs Adams, gently humming a hymn to herself, when she heard gunshots. She ran upstairs, armed with a fierce-looking kitchen knife. Bursting into the room wielding her weapon, she flicked the main light switch and saw Mr Adams with a gun in his hand and Mrs Adams in a pool of blood with gunshot wounds to her head. She screamed and ran downstairs, slamming the bedroom door behind her. She phoned the police. The police arrived in a matter of seconds (being a top politician they were never far away) to find Gene sat up in bed, still pointing the gun at the mirror, and staring at his bloody hand. They took him away and sent for an ambulance for his wife, but it was already too late for her.

Back on the moon the astronaut turned to Glen.

"The first stage is accomplished. My colleagues are arriving. It is time to begin the final stage. Prepare yourself for take-off; I will set the controls for the heart of the sun. We will set off as soon as the energy level is sufficient."

"What's that all about? The heart of the sun?" Glen asked.

"When this spaceship hits the heart of the sun the sun will explode and destroy the Earth."

"No, it won't, the ship isn't big enough. It will just burn up."

"It will contain the energy of my entire race and that will be enough to explode the sun. That is why we are waiting."

Glen strapped himself into his seat. He tried to interfere with the controls, but nothing seemed to work. He tried to contact the relay ship, but that didn't work either. He sat back and waited.

Back on earth people noticed that the sun was getting bigger. The air was getting hotter and hotter, until eventually the sun filled the entire sky and people were spontaneously bursting into flames, as were the objects around them. The seas and lakes and rivers boiled and evaporated quite quickly. Metal objects melted. No-one had a chance to do anything, as the whole process took a just couple of hours. And that was the end.

# Other books by Edwin Hird

## Rookery Villa and other strange tales

A collection of stories showing the impact ghosts and witches can have on normal people's lives. What can possibly go wrong when you're away on holiday? Then again, what can possibly go wrong when you stay at home?

*Rookery Villa* – Fiona and her family lose their home and go to stay with her mother until they find somewhere. But her childhood home has memories.

*Holiday Breakdown* – Two young couples from London are on holiday when their car breaks down in North Yorkshire. A jovial old lady offers them shelter until they get it repaired, and a little longer.

*The Big House* – Lizzie invites her best friend, Maddie, to spend a week with Aunty in her country mansion. Aunty turns out to be a bit stranger than Maddie expected.

*PW (in brackets)* – Four young women on a camping holiday come across the ruins of an ancient church. The church – and the nearby village – have dark pasts that come to the surface.

Available from Amazon

# Other books by Edwin Hird

## Cats in the Churchyard and other strange tales

A collection of stories showing the impact things from the dark side can have on normal people's lives. Unexpected events grab people from behind, and sometimes don't let go.

*Cats in the Churchyard* – Three young men come unstuck when they mess about with ancient local folklore. Their friends try to help, aided by two mysterious cats.

*Fear in the Workplace* – New girl Victoria is unsettled by her handsome colleague. "Why is it always cold around my desk?"

*Fog over the Pennines* – A coach pulls into a little hotel when the weather gets too bad to drive safely. But safety isn't what they find in this place.

*The Bike Ride* – Three young men on their weekly bike ride come across a derelict farmhouse and discover unexpected things in the neighbouring paddock.

*"You'll Like It Here"* – The residents of the old people's home are in surprisingly good health. Celia is invited to participate in their 'health scheme' but discovers more than they want her to know.

*Communications Meetings* – The new couple hold a séance to help Lydia come to terms with the recent death of her husband. Others 'invite' themselves, with unexpected consequences.

*Visiting Grandma* – Seventy-five years on and the virus is still with us. Some things remain the same; some things get worse.

Available from Amazon

# Other books by Edwin Hird

## Resurrection in the Crypt and other strange tales

A collection of stories showing strange things, or strange people, or strange circumstances, leading to unexpected events.

*Resurrection in the Crypt* – Felicity and her twin daughters travel to the other end of the country to help cousin Rosemary with Aunt Violet's funeral and discover dark family secrets.

*Grey Women and Wooden Men* – Justin and Danielle travel to a client out in the country, and strange dreams (or are they dreams?) come to life.

*23 Dunelm Terrace* – Sally and Ross move into their dream house, but it turns into a nightmare.

*The Sisters of the Village* – Hannah has some unexpected good luck when she inherits money and a house from an unknown relative. Her new life begins to take on a strange slant as she gets to know her new neighbours.

*Whispering Nights* – In Samantha's nightmare dreams her teddy bear comes to the rescue. Then she meets the dream characters in real life in the park.

*Mum's Chest* – Mum is struck by lightning and daughter Kate and son-in-law Tim are called to her bedside, only to discover it wasn't an accident.

*"The End is Nigh"* – Kevin carries his placard round central London to warn people of impending doom. Most people ignore him, but two unknowingly heed his warning.

Available from Amazon

# Other books by Edwin Hird

## Through the Ether and other strange tales

Another collection of stories of unusual things, people, or situations, with strange outcomes.

*Through the Ether* – A sequel to 'Cats in the Churchyard'. A psychic experiment has a strange outcome, with characters from past stories.

*The Travelling Bard* – Thomas goes from village to village telling stories and reciting poems to earn his crust. This time the weather upsets his plans.

*A Week in the Woods* – A school trip for bright children with poor practical skills goes wrong when one of the children brings external forces into play.

*Mystery in the Trees* – A large, glowing egg-shaped thing appears over the trees, and four musicians, a farmer and a police officer unexpectedly find themselves at a nearby country house.

*The Spare Room* – Martin moves in with his aunt and uncle to be near his new job. They put him up in the spare room, which no-one has stayed in before. Not for any length of time, anyway.

*The Body Shed* – Georgie's new house has some containers of dust in the shed; best friend Charlie's brother comes to stay and disturbs the peace.

Available from Amazon